TREASURE HUNTERS

THE GREATEST TREASURE HUNT

NO. 1 BESTSELLING AUTHOR

JAMES PATTERSON

and CHRIS GRABENSTEIN

Illustrated by JULIANA NEUFELD

001

Young Arrow
20 Vauxhall Bridge Road
London SW1V 2SA

Young Arrow is part of the Penguin Random House group of companies whose addresses can be found at global.penguinrandomhouse.com.

First published in the UK by Young Arrow in 2023

www.penguin.co.uk

A CIP catalogue record for this book is available from the British Library

ISBN: 978–1–529–12004–2

Printed and bound in Great Britain by Clays Ltd, Elcograf S.p.A.

Interior design by Tracy Shaw

The authorised representative in the EEA is Penguin Random House Ireland, Morrison Chambers, 32 Nassau Street, Dublin D02 YH68

www.greenpenguin.co.uk

Penguin Random House is committed to a sustainable future for our business, our readers and our planet. This book is made from Forest Stewardship Council® certified paper.

For Bailey and Logan Bigelow
—J. P.

ARCTIC OCEAN

GREENLAND

THE RIVER NENE IS THE TENTH-LONGEST RIVER IN THE UNITED KINGDOM AT ABOUT 100 MILES!

RIVER NENE

FRANCE

FRANCE IS THE MOST VISITED COUNTRY IN THE WORLD WITH ABOUT 90 MILLION TOURISTS EVERY YEAR!

ATLANTIC OCEAN

NORTH AMERICA

BORING, OREGON

COULD BE A GOOD PLACE TO VISIT IF WE NEED SOMEWHERE BORING AFTER A NEAR-DEATH ESCAPE!

CARTAGENA, SPAIN

AFRICA

CENTRAL AMERICA

SOUTH AMERICA

BALTIC SEA

POLAND

PIWNICA ŚWIDNICKA IN WROCŁAW, POLAND, IS THE OLDEST RESTAURANT IN EUROPE! IT'S BEEN AROUND SINCE ABOUT 1275—BUT DON'T WORRY. THE FOOD ISN'T 750 YEARS OLD.

RÜGEN, GERMANY

RÜGEN, THE LARGEST ISLAND IN GERMANY, IS FAMOUS FOR ITS WHITE-CHALK CLIFFS!

EUROPE

ASIA

MEDITERRANEAN SEA

THE SUEZ CANAL CREATED A FASTER PATH BETWEEN THE MEDITERRANEAN AND RED SEAS. IT IS LESS THAN 200 FEET WIDE AT ITS NARROWEST POINT. THAT'S WHAT I CALL A SHORTCUT!

PORT SAID, EGYPT

EVERY NOVEMBER, LOPBURI HAS A FESTIVAL TO CELEBRATE ITS MONKEYS. PEOPLE FEED MONKEYS LOTS OF YUMMY TREATS AND EVEN DRESS UP AS THEM!

LOPBURI, THAILAND

PACIFIC OCEAN

THE SAHARA DESERT

THE SAHARA DESERT IS THE WORLD'S LARGEST HOT DESERT—BUT JUST 6,000 YEARS AGO, IT WAS HOME TO RIVERS, LAKES, AND TROPICAL GRASSLANDS!

SUDAN

SUDAN HAS THE MOST PYRAMIDS IN THE WORLD—255. THAT'S ALMOST DOUBLE THE AMOUNT IN EGYPT!

INDIAN OCEAN

AUSTRALIA

NEW ZEALAND

ANTARCTICA

QUICK NOTE FROM BICK KIDD

Greetings, treasure hunters!

Bick (please-don't-call-me-Bickford-unless-you're-my-mom) Kidd here. Just wanted to remind you that I will be the one telling this story while my twin sister, Beck, (short for Rebecca, not Beckford) will be doing the illustrations.

Secondary quick note: if Beck draws me with lots of stink lines, that's what they call "artistic license" (also known as "not true").

I do bathe. I also brush my teeth. Whenever necessary.

Strangely, this tale of champions battling for glory doesn't start with an illustration of me, Beck, or our sibs, Storm and Tommy.

Nope. This story starts with some other kids treasure hunting.

The Collier kids!

UGH.

Just writing those three words makes me want to hurl!

PART ONE

LET THE GAMES BEGIN

CHAPTER 1

You know, I used to think that I was part of the greatest treasure-hunting family in the history of the world.

The Kidds!

(Maybe you've heard of us???)

But then I saw the Collier kids on YouTube.

Whoa. They're amazing. Like junior versions of Navy SEALs or Olympic gold medalists or those people on *American Ninja Warrior.* The ones who can bounce off the trampoline, swing on the flying nunchucks, run up the warped wall, and not even break a sweat. The ones who win.

The four of us Kidd kids were belowdecks on board our new ship, *The Lost Again.* We lost our first boat, *The Lost*—the one Beck, Storm, Tommy, and I all grew up on—when it sank into the Mediterranean Sea off the coast of Egypt after exploding into a ball of black smoke and roiling flames. (But that's another story.)

And you're right. *The Lost* was probably not the best name for a boat. Right up there with *The Sunk*, *The Doomed*, and *The Leaky Hull.* Let's hope *The Lost Again* doesn't get added to that list of stinkers anytime soon.

We were down in the galley, watching a video of the four Collier kids' most recent treasure-hunting adventure on their YouTube channel. While salvaging a long-lost Leonardo da Vinci painting from a flooded villa in Italy, they had to escape from modern-day, art-thieving pirates!

Every now and then, the show would cut to Nathan Collier doing commentary from his usual set on the Adventure Channel.

Yep. The four Collier kids were the children of Nathan Collier, Mom and Dad's number one nemesis. And, if he was back on YouTube and on the Adventure Channel, that meant he'd been released from prison in Peru. He had a fifth kid, another son, named Chet. Chet and Nathan were both put behind bars after they helped some loopy billionaire almost murder our big brother, Tommy, in a ritualistic sacrifice when we went searching for Paititi, the Lost City of Gold (which, of course, we found!). It almost became the City of Lost Tommy, too!

Nathan Collier was forever trying to snatch our finds or take credit for our discoveries because he wasn't very good at bringing anything up from a dive besides rusty hubcaps and seaweed.

But Collier still had his own basic cable show because he looked good on TV.

His four other kids, the ones not named Chet? They looked even better.

"Whoa," said Tommy, staring at the screen. "Is it just me, or do the Collier kids not look like they're even related?"

"Because," said Storm, pulling up data from her photographic memory and supercomputer brain, "Nathan Collier has had five different wives. Each of his children, including Chet, has a different mother."

"Check it out," I said, tapping the screen. "All four have Nathan Collier's signature spit curl over their left eyebrows."

"♫ *They are family* ♫," sang Beck. (BTW—she doesn't sing as good as she draws. Fine. She says I don't smell as good as she draws, either.)

Kirk, the oldest of the four, was their Tommy. Handsome. Sparkling smile. Muscles.

IT'S NOT BRAGGING IF YOU CAN BACK IT UP. 😎
AND IF YOU CAN'T BACK IT UP, YOU'RE NOT A COLLIER KID!
FOR REALS.
INDUBITABLY.
COLLIER KIDS QUEST!

Kioni was their Storm. The brains of the treasure-hunting team. In the video, she'd just used calculus and trigonometry to outfox the pirates. Something to do with tangents and vectors.

I guess twelve-year-old Carlos was a little like me. Maybe. Hard to say. I'd have to give him a good sniff.

They didn't really have a Beck. Maybe because they had a video crew following them around all day every day. They didn't need illustrations.

Nine-year-old Kaiyo Collier was the youngest. We didn't have a Kaiyo in our crew. I was kind of glad. The kid could be extremely snarky.

For instance, after they outran the pirates chasing their boat by doing some circus-level acrobatics and trapeze action on the rigging of their ship, Kaiyo grabbed a bullhorn and blasted them with her 'tude.

"I see you guys set aside this special time to humiliate yourselves in public."

I think she hurt the pirates' feelings.

After she mocked them, the Roger on their flag didn't look so Jolly.

CHAPTER 2

"Well done, children," Nathan Collier told his four kids as the episode wrapped up. He looked right at the camera and continued. "A da Vinci painting just like this one sold for four hundred and fifty million dollars at a New York City auction back in 2017."

"That was the highest price ever paid for a painting," reported Kioni, just like Storm would've if we were the ones who'd found the oil painting.

"Ja," said Kirk, giving his blond spit curl a finger flick. "The highest price ever paid for a painting...until we sell this one!"

"We're gonna be rich," said Carlos. "No. Check

that. We're gonna be richer. Time to buy that second Maserati!"

Carlos slapped his big brother a high five.

"You guys, what's the big deal?" said Kaiyo sarcastically. "It's easy to find money. It's in every dictionary."

The other Colliers tossed back their heads and laughed.

Storm rolled her eyes and swiped away the video clip.

"Whoa," said Tommy when Storm cut the streaming feed. "Aren't you going to give 'em a thumbs-up and hit the Subscribe button?"

"No, Tommy," said Storm, "I am not going to do either of those things. Everyone knows that the da Vinci painting they're talking about, a work called *Salvator Mundi*, the one that sold for all those millions, turned out to be a fake and an embarrassment to the prince who purchased it."

"You think the one the Collier kids found is a fake, too?" wondered Beck.

"It's a definite possibility. It might even be the *same* fake painting."

"Doesn't matter," I said. "It made for a great episode. Action. Adventure. Suspense. Pirates. Pizza."

"Totally," said Tommy. "By the way—does that Kirk dude have bigger guns than me?" He flexed his arms to pump up his biceps.

We all ignored Tommy's question because he's our big brother and we didn't want to hurt his feelings. But if Tommy's arms were mighty oaks, Kirk Collier's were giant sequoias.

"That should be *us* on YouTube!" I whined.

"I'd design way better graphics," said Beck. "By the way—is that little kid Kaiyo supposed to be me? She's so annoying."

"And you're not," I said, making sure it in no way sounded like a question.

"I take issue with some of Kioni's use of the Pythagorean theorem in her triangulation efforts," said Storm.

"How about Kirk's chin dimple?" asked Tommy. "Is it deeper than mine?"

Mom and Dad came into the galley. They were hauling scuba gear.

"What are you guys doing down here?" asked Mom.

"Checking out the Collier kids on YouTube," I said. "They dropped a fresh episode today."

Dad chuckled. "Your mother and I find your fascination with these young YouTube stars to be rather amusing. It's just another one of Nathan Collier's cheap gimmicks. Another publicity stunt."

"Collier isn't a serious treasure hunter," said Mom. "He's not in it for the right reason—advancing the study of archaeology or celebrating the artistic merit of his found artifacts. He just wants the fame and glory that comes from making a big find."

"And the money," added Dad. "Collier's always enjoyed the money."

"True," said Mom.

Dad pointed at our laptop. "Kids? Staring at your screens all day isn't the most productive use of your time. Especially since we have serious, real-world treasure hunting of our own to do."

"Are you guys forgetting why we're docked

here off the coast of Spain?" asked Mom. "We're very close to finding the long-lost sarcophagus of Pharaoh Menkaure!"

"Yeah," I said, putting a hand to my ear. "I think I hear his mummy calling us."

I was trying to pull a Kaiyo. To be the funny one in the family.

It wasn't working. The Colliers would've yukked it up for the cameras, but nobody in my family was tossing back their heads and laughing.

CHAPTER 3

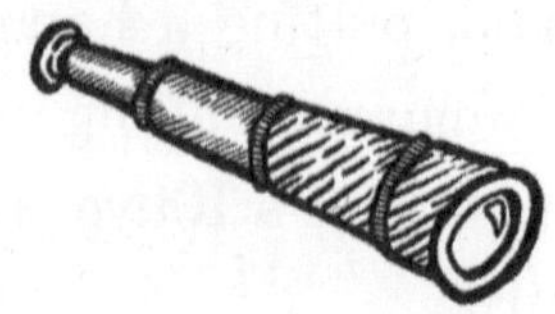

Tommy, Beck, and I pulled on our scuba gear. Storm never went on dives with us. "Someone has to stay with the ship," she'd say. She also didn't like wearing the snug, rubbery wet suits. "They chafe."

We'd docked in the Mediterranean Sea off the coast of Cartagena, Spain. Mom and Dad had a lead on a British ship called the *Beatrice* that sank in 1838. It had been carrying the sarcophagus of Pharaoh Menkaure from Egypt to the British Museum in England.

Storm, of course, knew all the details and had filled us in the night before.

"The sarcophagus, or, in this case, the beautiful

black basalt stone coffin, had been removed—some would say stolen—by British adventurers seeking treasure deep inside the burial chambers of Egypt's Giza pyramids. They'd used dynamite to blast their way through the stone block walls in their quest to find ancient artifacts."

We all exchanged glances when Storm mentioned the pyramids. We'd had a few adventures of our own inside them when we went on a journey down the Nile.

"Was the ship cursed by Menkaure's mummy?" Tommy asked, his eyes wide.

"It sank, didn't it?" said Beck.

I added a spooky "moo-ha-ha" that creeped Tommy out. We were double-teaming him. It's a twin thing.

Anyway, now we were going to dive into the Mediterranean Sea to see if we could retrieve the sarcophagus that'd been lying at the bottom for almost two centuries.

"I'm taking my dive camera!" I told Beck.

"I'm grabbing one, too!" she replied. "I'll illustrate our underwater adventures with it!"

"We can become famous YouTube stars, just like the Collier kids!" I exclaimed.

I might've exclaimed that a little too loudly. Because Mom and Dad were giving me and Beck a seriously disappointed look.

"*Nisi utile est quod facimus,*" said Mom, our onboard classic languages instructor.

"*Stulta est gloria,*" added Dad, finishing her thought.

"That's a quote from Phaedrus," said Storm.

"Was Phaedrus like a pharaoh?" asked Tommy.

Storm shook her head. "No, Tommy. Phaedrus was a first-century Roman who translated Aesop's fables into Latin."

"Can you translate his quotation, Stephanie?" said Mom, in full-on Latin teacher mode. And, yes, Stephanie is Storm's real name. Double yes—Mom and Dad are the only ones who can call her that without Storm exploding into a tsunami.

Storm pointed a finger to the bright-blue sky, as if she were a marble statue of a Roman scholar and told us what Mom and Dad had been trying to say: "Unless what we do is useful, glory is foolish."

"In other words," said Dad, "being famous for the sake of being famous is a colossal waste of time, kids."

"We have more important work to do," said Mom. "Because true glory lies in noble deeds."

Beck and I both nodded like we understood. We even put on sad puppy-dog faces to show we'd learned our lesson and wouldn't pee on the carpet again.

But when Mom and Dad weren't looking, we

tucked our underwater cameras into our dive bags.

We were going to let those YouTubing Collier kids know that we were just as good as they were.

No. We were better!

We were the Kidd kids!

We jumped into the water. It was showtime!

CHAPTER 4

Like always, Mom and Dad had aced their homework assignment.

The *Beatrice* shipwreck was right where they predicted it would be. They gave us a series of underwater hand gestures and led the way toward the sunken ship's cargo hold. The hand signals told us to "follow" them.

We all gave them the classic "okay" gesture, which, by the way, is the same thumb-and-fingers thing underwater as it is on dry land. (Just in case you ever want to signal "okay" in the bathtub or a swimming pool.)

Mom and Dad kicked off and disappeared into a cloud of foamy bubbles.

We swam behind them.

Until I saw this cool-looking gash in the deck of the ship. I knew it'd make an awesome background for a dramatic action scene.

I signaled to Beck to pull out her camera. I was going to pretend that my leg was stuck between two jagged boards and something scary was swimming straight at me. I figured I could search online for some stock shark footage and do a cool edit to make it look like I was trapped but fighting off a shark attack. That would definitely get the Likes and Loves flying on our video when we posted it.

I squeezed my leg into the spiky gash and started flailing my arms around.

Beck gave me a big thumbs-up, like the ones I hoped this video clip would generate. She was recording it, and it was looking awesome.

Tommy saw me playing to the camera, so he swam over to join in.

First, he did a bodybuilder pose. Then he grabbed on to my arm and started tugging. I pretended like I was still stuck. I gave the "danger over there" hand signal to really sell the shark attack.

Tommy yanked. I pulled back like I was still stuck. He yanked again. We had a great back-and-forth rhythm going. This would be an awesome action sequence. Especially when we added in the dramatic DUN-DUN-DUN music.

Finally, Tommy gave me one last heave. To sell the rescue, I pushed off the deck of the shipwreck hard. We shot away from the *Beatrice*. Beck almost lost her camera when she gave us an excited double thumbs-up. We'd nailed the scene!

That's when we heard the creaking.

And the groaning.

Apparently, all that back-and-forth, pull-push action—combined with my overly dramatic push-off—had dislodged the rotting wooden ship from its resting spot. It started teetering and tottering and tearing itself apart.

With Mom and Dad down in the cargo hold!

Just as I started to seriously panic and hyperventilate (which, BTW, is never a great idea when you're *underwater*) I spotted two very familiar forms swimming toward us.

Mom and Dad!

They'd both just scissor kicked their way out of a hatch and were once again signaling for us to follow them. Their hand gestures seemed a little angrier than they had been the first time.

They both jabbed a finger to their temples. The universal sign for "Think!" The jab was so hard, it added the exclamation point.

Mom used both hands to draw a rectangle in the water, then gestured down.

They'd found the sarcophagus! They needed help hauling it back up to the surface.

Tommy, Beck, and I swam toward Mom and Dad.

They gave us more hand gestures, outlining our part in the salvage job. We were ready to get busy. I kind of hoped it would also make Mom and Dad forget how we'd been goofing around and rocking the boat.

That's when the unsteady shipwreck heaved into a lurch and collapsed on itself, sending up swirls of murky water and debris. My dramatic kickoff had jostled the *Beatrice* so much, it'd started sinking again!

We watched in horror. The sarcophagus that'd

been lost for so long was on its way to being lost forever.

But sinking the *Beatrice* wasn't even our biggest blunder. Some even bigger problems were headed our way because our frantic fake action had also stirred up an ugly scorpion fish attack!

Yes, the attack *and* the fish were both extremely UGLY!

CHAPTER 5

Okay, a lot of this scorpion fish stuff I learned later—after we survived the sneak attack and Storm gave me the scary data dump.

The ugly thing's prey hardly ever see the scorpion fish's attack coming because scorpion fish are excellent at blending in with their surroundings—looking like rocks, coral reefs, or sunken cargo ships.

They have wide, ginormous mouths, which means they can suck in and swallow their prey with one big gulp (and not the kind they sell at 7-Eleven). They're also some of the most poisonous fish in the sea. Their sharp, spiky spines? Think prickly porcupine quills loaded with venom. They might as well call them the poison dart fish.

One of the scorpion fish jabbed Tommy in the ankle.

I think Tommy yelped when he got stung. A whole bunch of bubbles came gurgling out around his regulator mouthpiece when the fish poked him. I guess that's how you scream "YOUCH!" when you're underwater.

After Beck and I did some serious arm flailing and leg kicking, the other two scorpion fish fled. They might've seen our terrified faces, too. Magnified by our diving masks, we looked even uglier than the big-mouthed monster fish.

All this scorpion fish action was going on while the wreck of the *Beatrice* continued to snap timbers and cave in on itself. Mom and Dad signaled for us to leave the wreck immediately, if not sooner. Debris was tumbling all around us. The water became a murky cloud of stirred-up sand. We had to abandon any plans we had for salvaging the pharaoh's sarcophagus.

(Mom and Dad might've also abandoned any plans they had for sending their children to college.)

Our parental units looked very, very upset. And by upset, I mean they were angry, annoyed, and infuriated—plus about two dozen other words for being ticked off and bent out of shape.

By horsing around, mugging for Beck's camera (which she wasn't even supposed to be carrying), Tommy and I had totally wrecked the shipwreck expedition.

People had been searching for the *Beatrice* for over a century. We found it. Then, we totally buried it in its own debris. I felt horrible. So did Beck. It's another twin thing.

I looked over at Tommy.

He was gripping his ankle. When he took away his gloved hands, I could see that his lower leg was swollen.

In fact, it had inflated to the size of a small birthday balloon. His puffed-out, bloated ankle might act like a fishline bobber and float him up to the surface, flippers-first.

Tommy pointed to himself with one finger, then poked his wrist with the same finger. It was the underwater signal for "I've been stung and need to go up top for some first aid treatment."

Then he put both hands together in a praying gesture. That's the universal symbol for "Please?!?"

Mom and Dad each grabbed hold of one of Tommy's arms.

They scissor kicked and rocketed him up to the surface through a swirling cloud of tiny air bubbles. Beck and I shot up right after them, completely abandoning any ideas we might've had about recording more underwater footage for our YouTube debut.

The whole time we were swimming for the surface, I wondered if our wannabe YouTube antics would cost Tommy his leg, maybe his life.

And did those same antics cost the world the sarcophagus of Pharaoh Menkaure?

That made me feel terrible.

We were supposed to be treasure hunters and treasure finders.

Not treasure losers.

CHAPTER 6

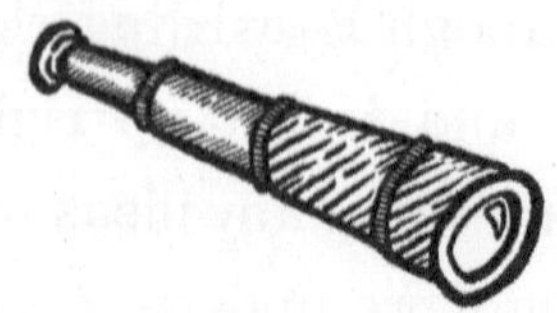

Fortunately, we have one extremely awesome first aid kit aboard *The Lost Again.*

The thing even has lollipops to give to good patients. Tommy asked for a red one.

He was going to be okay.

"But zoom in on my ankle, Beck!" he said. "Before the swelling goes down. This scorpion fish sting would definitely make for awesome, must-see TV."

Beck almost pulled out her camera to get the shot.

But then she saw the extremely disappointed looks on Mom's and Dad's faces. She probably also heard the tsk-tsking of their tongues.

"Kids?" said Dad. "Your behavior on this dive was very disheartening."

Mom joined in on the chorus: "You were acting like children!"

Um, we are children, I almost said. But here's the thing: we Kidds have never acted like kids. We've always been self-reliant. We know how to take care of ourselves and our ship. In fact, for a pretty long stretch of time, when Dad was missing and Mom was kidnapped, we had zero adult supervision. We *had* to take care of ourselves. We wouldn't have survived if we'd acted like needy children.

So that was probably the absolute worst thing our parents could've called us. Even if we deserved it, which, hello, we did.

"We're sorry," Beck and I mumbled together.

"Chya," added Tommy. "Totally. We didn't mean to, you know, wreck the shipwreck."

Storm shook her head. She was disappointed in us, too.

"I'm so glad I don't do dives," she muttered.

"Especially the ones that end in disaster and disillusioned family members."

Mom threw up both arms in frustration. "We can't believe that you three are more interested in becoming YouTube stars than salvaging a treasure that has been lost since 1838! That's nearly two centuries!"

"And," added Storm, "Pharoah Menkaure of the Fourth Dynasty of the Old Kingdom died around 2500 BC. That means the three-ton stone relic down below is over four thousand years old! Show it some respect, people."

"You three are grounded," said Dad.

Tommy had a confused look on his face. "Like, here on the boat?"

"Exactly."

"Um, can you be grounded if there's no, you know, ground? Just seawater? I guess we could be 'decked' since we're standing on a deck..."

"You're being punished, Tommy," said Mom. "You, too, Bick and Beck. No screen time. No snacks."

Storm raised her hand.

Mom nodded. She didn't need to hear the question. "You're not being punished, Stephanie. You may still have access to the snack cabinets."

"And the Oreos?"

"Yes," said Dad. "But kindly save one sleeve of the Double Stuf ones for me."

Storm gave him a thumbs-up. "You got it."

Dad turned to Tommy. "Thomas?"

"Yes, sir?"

"Can you remain focused long enough to operate the winch?"

"Sure."

"Mom and I are going back down. We might be able to wrap the cable around the sarcophagus and haul it up to the surface."

"If we can still find it under all that rubble," said Mom.

Dad nodded. "We think we can. It won't be easy. But few things worth doing are. When we have the relic secured, we'll signal you to start hoisting it up."

"It'll be heavy," said Mom. "As Storm mentioned, it's three tons of stone."

"Plus," said Storm, "it's waterlogged. And every gallon of water inside the sarcophagus will weigh eight point three four pounds."

Tommy nodded. "Got it. Thanks for the heads-up, Storm."

"Stand by, Thomas," said Dad.

"Standing by, sir," Tommy replied with a salute. He realized he was still sucking on his red lollipop and plucked it out of his mouth. "And I promise not to do anything childish."

"We can help Tommy," I offered.

"We're good at belaying stuff with grappling hooks," added Beck.

"And," I said, "we know how to handle precious cargo without scratching it."

Mom and Dad both gave us a look.

"Oh," said Mom, "you mean like that precious cargo ship down below that you not only scratched but totally demolished?"

"That was a one-off," Beck tried. "A mistake."

"And like you guys are always saying," I told them, "we learn from our mistakes, not our successes." Yes, I was going with the "butter up Mom and Dad" move. It wasn't working.

Dad gave me his narrow-eyed "I'm still disappointed" look.

"We don't want to tempt fate," he said. "Tommy and Storm can handle the extraction chores at this end. You two stay down below in your cabins. Maybe meditate on what happened earlier."

Youch. That stung worse than a scorpion fish's fin. Mom and Dad were sending us to our rooms to think about what we'd done. Nothing will make you feel more like a child than that.

Our disappointed parents grabbed fresh oxygen tanks, pulled down their masks, and dove back into the water, dragging the hook end of the winch cable with them. Tommy monitored the line feed off the spool. Storm was standing by to assist in any way possible.

Beck and I slumped our shoulders and headed to our cabins.

As we passed through the deckhouse (it's sort of the ship's living room), I heard a *ding* and noticed an incoming email message on our family computer.

It was an invitation. From Nathan Collier.

Greetings, Thomas and Sue.

Nathan Collier here. I know we've had our differences in the past, and believe me when I say I'm sorry about that unfortunate misunderstanding down in Peru! But in the spirit of promoting and advancing the study of archaeology, which I know we all love, I'm hoping your four children—Tommy, Storm, Bick, and Beck—will appear in an action-packed adventure series with four of my children—Kirk, Kioni, Carlos, and Kaiyo. It would be a special, heavily promoted competition on YouTube and the Adventure Channel entitled *The World's Greatest Treasure-Hunting Kids!*

Please meet us when you arrive in London with the British Museum's long-lost sarcophagus (I know you're close to salvaging it) to discuss this glorious and highly educational adventure series! My lawyers can work out all the nitty-gritty details. I have very good lawyers.

Sincerely,
Nathan Collier
The World's Most Famous (Adult) Treasure Hunter

CHAPTER 7

Beck and I have cabins across the hall from each other.

With both our doors wide open, and still smarting from Mom and Dad calling us *children*, it was very easy for us to launch into Twin Tirade number 2,132.

Tirades are supposed to be long, angry speeches filled with furious criticism and angry accusations. Our Twin Tirades, on the other hand, are typically short. Like a thin scrap of paper that flares up in a firepit with a burst of heat and light and fiery red embers along the edges and then, almost immediately, crinkles into a floating clump of wispy black soot that's

colder than a falling leaf during pumpkin spice season.

"Why'd you tell me to dive with a camera?" Beck shouted out her door.

"This isn't my fault, Beck!" I hollered back at her. "Why'd you dive with a camera?"

"Because, Bickford, you asked me to!"

"If I asked you to eat worms, would you?"

"Earthworms are a superfood, Bick. They're high in protein and have mega levels of iron and amino acids!"

"They also make me want to hurl!"

"So does your face, Bick, but I deal with it."

"We're twins, Beck, remember? Our faces are very similar."

"That's true," said Beck. "So, if I asked *you* to jump off a cliff, would you?"

"Maybe," I said. "If I had a hang glider."

"Or if there was a zip line," said Beck.

"That'd be awesome. Like that time in South America."

"Yeah. We should do that again sometime."

"Definitely. The next time we're near a cliff."

And just like that, we were done. Which was a good thing. Because up on the deck, we heard the WHIRR-CLINK-CLICK of the winch hauling something heavy up from down below.

Mom and Dad must've been able to snag the sarcophagus!

CHAPTER 8

Beck and I bolted out of our rooms and raced up to the deck to lend a hand.

It's what we Kidds do best. We help one another out. Like they say, teamwork makes the dream work.

The black stone coffin emerged from the water with a mighty SPLOOSH.

"Easy," Storm coached Tommy. "Easy."

"Got it," said Tommy, who's an expert at operating anything and everything on board *The Lost Again*. When we four were on our own, he was definitely our captain. By the way, our parents sometimes call him Tailspin Tommy. Not because

I THINK I'M IN LOVE WITH YONDER MERMAID! NO, WAIT. THAT'S A GIANT SQUID.
I'VE HEARD OF A BURIAL AT SEA. THIS MUST BE THE OPPOSITE.
CRANK

they've seen him fly, which, if you're his passenger, is a great way to lose your lunch while he executes a few barrel rolls and loop the loops. No, they gave him that nickname because he goes into a tailspin and falls head over heels in love on a regular basis. Like every time he meets or sees a pretty girl. Tommy has tumbled into love so often he needs about ten dozen of those frilly heart-shaped cards every Valentine's Day.

"Um, can this ship really handle another three tons?" I asked as we slowly lowered the black basalt box to the deck.

"We're safely inside our gross load capacity," said Storm confidently.

"Really?" said Beck. "Even with Bick on board? Have you seen the way he eats? It's extremely gross. Way over the limit."

I just laughed. Busting chops? That's another thing tight families do.

The sarcophagus was incredible. Not just because it was an amazing work of intricately sculpted art but because of the story it told. The history it contained. There are all kinds of treasures in the world, I guess. Gold, silver, precious jewels. But the ancient artifacts, the time travelers? Those are the ones worth finding and keeping so you can keep their history alive for all time.

When our precious cargo was secure and strapped down, Mom and Dad climbed up the ladder to the deck and peeled back their dive masks.

They were smiling again. Our salvage mission was a success. I think they were also happy to see us all working together to save this Egyptian treasure.

"Well done, everybody," boomed Dad. "As you can see, all was not lost down below. Our friends in Egypt will be delighted when we return this to them."

Storm looked confused—a very rare occurrence, by the way.

"We're not taking it to the British Museum?" she said. "That's where the cargo ship known as the *Beatrice* was originally transporting it."

Mom shook her head. "No, Storm. We've been communicating with the folks at UNESCO."

UNESCO isn't the cookie baking company. (That's Nabisco.) It's the United Nations Educational, Scientific and Cultural Organization.

"Their committee for promoting the return of cultural property to its country of origin has already ruled," Mom continued. "We're taking this treasure back to where it came from and where it still belongs. Egypt. Maybe they'll even put it on display near the Giza pyramids where it was supposed to rest for all time."

Beck and I exchanged a quick glance.

We weren't as happy or giddy as we had been a few seconds earlier.

Because if we were really heading to Egypt instead of sailing on to England, we wouldn't be able to meet with Nathan Collier in London to discuss his cool idea for a treasure-hunting tournament against the Collier kids!

And that was something we really, really wanted to do.

CHAPTER 9

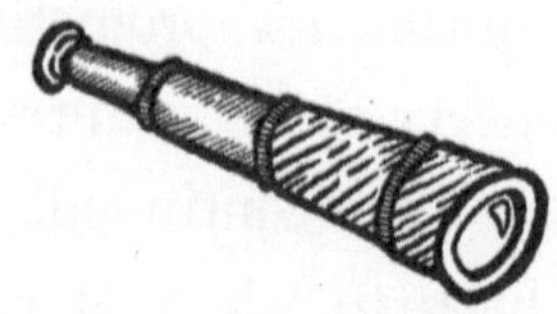

We set sail for Port Said, an Egyptian city on the coast of the Mediterranean Sea, just north of the Suez Canal.

"Do you think the others saw the message from Nathan Collier?" I asked Beck as we worked the ropes, cables, and chains to rig *The Lost Again*'s sails for the journey east.

"If they didn't," said Beck, "we can show it to them. I printed out a hard copy."

"Smart thinking."

"Yeah," said Beck, giving me a little side eye. "I find that's the best kind of thinking to do. The smart kind."

When we were underway, we convened a quick

Kidd kid meeting up in the wheelhouse with Tommy and Storm.

"Collier and his kids are challenging us to a duel!" I said. "But, instead of pistols or swords, we'll need to use our treasure-hunting skills as our weapons."

"No problemo," said Beck. "It's what we do best."

"What sort of challenges might this competition include?" asked Storm.

Beck shrugged. "That part's pretty vague. But we should definitely hear Collier out."

"Seriously?" said Tommy. "Isn't this the same Collier dude who, along with his skeevy son Chet, basically tried to have me killed in Peru?"

"Chet's out of the picture," I said.

"Maybe yours," said Tommy. "I still have thought bubbles about him."

"Look, Tommy, if we don't accept this challenge, Kirk, Kioni, Carlos, and Kaiyo Collier are gonna be all over YouTube trashing us and calling us chickens."

Beck wiped her face. I'd just given her a spittle shower. "Do you really have to put so much oomph behind all those *k* sounds, Bick?"

"Sorry."

"Did any of you guys notice how many muscles that Kirk guy has?" said Tommy. "Even his knuckles bulge."

"The most important muscle to exercise, Tommy," said Storm, "is the one between your ears."

"Totally," said Tommy. "That's the one I use to wiggle my eyebrows when I meet a pretty lady."

"I was talking about your brain, Tommy!" said

Storm. "That's what we'll need to beat these new Collier kids!"

"Nah," said Tommy. "We won't need my brain, Storm. We've got yours."

Storm blushed a little.

"You guys?" I said. "We're not going to get a chance to challenge the Colliers unless Mom and Dad say we can do it."

"So go ask them," said Tommy.

"That would be the logical first step," added Storm.

"Okay," I said, mustering up my courage. "We'll do it."

"Right now!" said Beck. Guess she'd mustered up some courage, too.

We dashed down the wheelhouse steps and headed belowdecks.

We could hear Mom's and Dad's voices. They were up front, in The Room. Apparently, they'd left The Door open.

Yes, every time any of us talk about The Room or The Door to The Room (which is five-inch-thick solid steel with a serious dead bolt like you'd find in a bank vault), it always comes out sounding like we're talking in capital letters. The Room is where Mom and Dad keep the most secret stuff on the boat. Treasure maps. Retrieval plans. Notes on dealers and go-betweens for museums.

"Why'd they leave The Door open?" Beck whispered.

I shrugged and placed a finger to my lips. It was time to do a little eavesdropping. Okay. We were going to spy on our parents.

Hey, they both used to be spies, for the CIA. Who do you think we learned it from?

CHAPTER 10

"Here's the file for Königsberg Castle," we heard Mom say.

"Thanks, Sue," said Dad, sounding sort of down.

"Cheer up, Tom," said Mom. "No treasure has to remain lost forever. We just proved that today."

"But what about my grandfather's reputation?" said Dad. "That was lost back in 1945. And no matter how hard we try, how much good we do by returning lost treasures to their rightful owners, we can never truly redeem the Kidd family name until we solve the mystery of Joseph Kidd and Königsberg Castle."

Whoa, I thought. *Breaking News Alert. Our family name needs redemption?*

That meant somebody up in the branches of our family tree did something seriously bad or wrong (maybe our great-grandfather Joseph Kidd, who might not've been so great after all). And it happened at Königsberg Castle.

"I'm sure there is a reasonable explanation,"

EVERY FAMILY TREE HAS SOME LEMONS, SOME NUTS, AND A FEW BAD APPLES.

Mom told Dad. "And, one day, we'll find it, Thomas. I know we will."

"We have to," said Dad. "Otherwise, everything we've done, all the lost treasures we've found, all the artwork we've returned to its rightful homes, all of it will be for nothing."

Whoa, I thought. *What was this big family secret? And why hadn't anybody told us about it?*

Beck knuckle punched me in my arm. Guess I was doing too much thinking when we should be helping Dad deal with whatever it was about Great-Grandpa Joe that'd been bugging him since, well, probably all the way back to when *he* was a kid and first learned about whatever bad thing his grandfather had done.

So, even though The Room was Off-Limits, we rapped our knuckles on that open thick steel door.

That startled Mom and Dad.

They very quickly and very smoothly tucked whatever papers they'd been studying back into their file folders.

"Hi, guys," said Dad with a nervous smile. "Do you need something?"

"Not really," said Beck, because she, like me, clearly felt that a made-for-YouTube treasure-hunting competition with the Collier kids wasn't nearly as important as fixing whatever had been bugging Dad his whole life.

But we couldn't let on that we'd been spying on Mom and Dad's conversation. Sure, we wanted to solve the mystery of our great-grandfather's goof-up. But we couldn't just start blurting out questions about something we weren't supposed to even know about.

"So," I said, as nonchalantly as I could, "we saw The Door was open..."

"Your father had boiled cabbage for lunch," said Mom.

"Half a cup has one-third of all the vitamin C you need for the day," said Dad proudly.

"Cool," I said. "So, what're you guys working on?"

"Nothing really," said Mom.

"Just a puzzle we've been pondering," added Dad. "Some mental gymnastics to help pass the time as we make our way east to Egypt."

Still smiling, Dad deftly slipped all the file folders into a small metal box, closed the lid, and spun its combination lock to seal it.

Oh, yeah.

He was definitely hiding something from us.

CHAPTER 11

Sailing the 1,700 nautical miles from where we were off the coast of Cartagena, Spain, to Port Said, Egypt, at a speed of ten knots would take us about seven days.

A whole week.

So, Mom and Dad would have plenty of time to ponder their puzzle. They could also probably piece together seven different jigsaw puzzles. They might even have time to bake a bunch of sourdough bread.

Sailboats, even souped-up ones like *The Lost Again*, just aren't as fast as planes, trains, or automobiles.

Tommy, Storm, Beck, and I did everything we needed to do to keep our ship clipping along. We also stayed up on our boat school lessons. (That's kind of like home school when your house is a boat.) But that never took all day. And we weren't very big on jigsaw puzzles. Or baking sourdough bread.

We did do as much research as we could into Königsberg Castle, drilling down to the "Storm Is the Only One Who Cares" level with stuff like learning that the site of the castle was originally an Old Prussian fort known as Tuwangste near the Pregel River at an important waypoint in Prussian territory.

But we couldn't find anything about Dad's grandpa.

We also spent a bunch of time checking out more Collier kid videos on YouTube.

One we watched really made us mad.

"We're here in Peru!" said hunky Kirk.

"One of the five cradles of civilization," added the brainy Kioni. "Former home of the Incan Empire. Peru has a population of thirty-three million. Its capital and largest city is Lima."

"Just like the beans!" snarked Kaiyo, the youngest.

"Her facts are dull and boring," said Storm, giving her honest critique. "Like an elementary school geography report. *She's* dull and boring. And her little sister, Kaiyo, is worse. She's annoying."

Have I mentioned that my big sister doesn't have much of a filter? She says whatever's on her mind whenever it happens to be there.

"I think brainy Kioni is kind of a cutie," said Tommy, using that muscle between his ears to wiggle-waggle his eyebrows.

Now Carlos, the Collier kid who was the same age as Beck and me, addressed the camera.

"Guys, we've marched and macheted our way through the Amazon Rain Forest to find this!" He gestured dramatically for the camera to pan to the right. "Paititi! The Lost City of Gold!"

Our jaws all dropped.

"Colliers!" I said, once again spitting out the *k* sound.

Beck didn't mind this time. Because *we* were the ones who'd discovered Paititi, the Lost City

of Gold. That's where Nathan Collier and his cronies almost had Tommy murdered in that bizarre sacrificial ritual.

"Fake!" I shouted, poking my finger at the screen.

"That's not the City of Gold!" screamed Beck. "It can't be. The local extraction team dismantled it."

"And," said Storm, "all the gold went to fund

a trust for rain forest protection that Mom set up with the president of Peru!"

Tommy practically put his nose to the screen. "Check it out. Look at all the teeny-tiny people in the temple!"

Beck and I both snapped our fingers.

"Of course!" I said.

"Green screen!" said Beck.

"That's the model!"

"From the Smithsonian!"

"The exhibit!"

"The display Mom and Dad constructed."

"About the Lost City."

"Of Paititi!"

We slapped each other a high five. This was something new we'd been doing. Instead of a Twin Tirade, it was a Twin Brainstorm. Number 17, to be precise.

"Fascinating," said Storm. "They faked the whole thing. That jungle they were chopping their way through wasn't the Amazon Rain Forest. It was probably a collection of garden plants they ordered from Amazon and set up in their backyard!"

"Colliers!" Beck and I said together. And, yes, we both spit out the *k*.

"They're phonies," said Storm.

"Chya," said Tommy. "But they're also famous."

"Which means people will believe them over us," I said.

"Unless we defeat them in the treasure hunter tournament!"

"What treasure hunter tournament?"

It was Mom.

She and Dad had just joined us in the galley.

CHAPTER 12

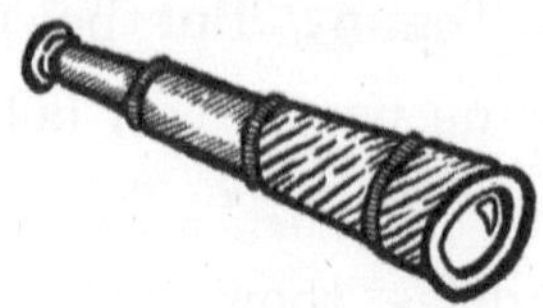

We were about to explain the whole "World's Greatest Treasure-Hunting Kids" concept when Nathan Collier came on the screen to do it for us.

"Thanks, Kirk, Kioni, Carlos, and Kaiyo Collier!" he said. Then he wiped the lens of the camera with his sleeve. All those *k* sounds kick up a rain forest of their own, no matter who's spraying them when they're saying them.

Collier was sitting in a stuffed chair and sipping tea in what looked like some kind of Explorers' Club in jolly old England.

"As you can clearly see, my children are the best young treasure hunters in the world. No

other...*kids*...can hunt treasure like my *kids*: Kirk, Kioni, Carlos, and Kaiyo. My ex-wives and I are very proud of our four *kids*!"

The video finally ended.

"Why is Nathan Collier not still in jail?" was Mom's first reaction.

"He must know some very important people," said Dad.

"Or extremely sleazy ones," replied Mom.

"I did some quick research," reported Storm. "His lawyers were able to have his sentence reduced to mandatory public service because he wasn't the one holding the knife when they were attempting to remove Tommy's still-beating heart with a jagged blade in their simulation of the Incan ritual."

Tommy's knees went a little wobbly. "Whew. Not so many descriptive details, please."

"Sorry," said Storm. "Sometimes a photographic memory can be a curse."

"Chya!"

"In the small victories department," Storm continued, "Collier's oldest son, Chet, remains behind bars. The lawyers weren't interested in springing him. This YouTube show with his four other children? It, apparently, is considered part of Nathan Collier's service to the public."

"You're joking," said Mom.

Storm shook her head. "I wish I were. As I said, Mr. Collier had some very good and extremely expensive lawyers."

Dad stroked his beard thoughtfully. "In that video clip we just watched, Collier certainly repeated the word *kid* an awful lot."

"Because," I said, "he wants us, the Kidd kids, to take on his children in a televised competition."

"What?" said Mom.

Beck handed Mom the printout of Collier's message. Dad leaned in to read along with her.

"A treasure-hunting tournament?" said Mom after taking in what Collier had suggested.

I nodded. "The four of us against the four of them. The Kidd kids versus the Collier kids."

Beck shook her head. "I can't believe they're seriously telling the world that they, not us, found the Lost City of Paititi in Peru!"

"Me neither," I said. "I think they're trying to smear our family's name and reputation."

That punched Dad's buttons, big time. His whole face went red with rage. I thought his beard might catch on fire.

Mom placed a gentle hand on his shoulder.

"This is what Collier has always done, Thomas," she said, her voice calm and soothing.

"He lets us do all the hard work and research. Then he swoops in, claims credit, and grabs all the media attention."

"But everybody knows we were the ones who found the Lost City of Gold!" Dad insisted. "We even did an exhibit at the Smithsonian about it!"

"Unfortunately," said Storm, "the audience for internet videos doesn't spend much time visiting museums." She gestured toward the laptop screen. "This is the only 'truth' they will ever see."

"But Collier is a terrible treasure hunter," said Dad, shaking his head in frustrated disbelief. "He couldn't find his way out of a maze if all the rats and mice helped him!"

"Totally," said Tommy, piling on. "Collier couldn't pour water out of a boot with a hole in the toe and directions on the heel."

That made Dad smile. Finally.

"Well, Kidds," said Dad, regaining his cool, "maybe this 'tournament' Mr. Collier's proposing would be a good thing. We can use *his* media platform to show the world what true archaeology and treasure hunting is all about."

“We can also stop them from trash-talking us,” said Tommy.

“Agreed,” said Storm. “We need to protect our family’s good name!”

“Yes,” said Dad, sounding like his mind was drifting back to wherever it was when he and Mom were talking about his grandfather in The Room. “We certainly do need to do that, Storm.”

CHAPTER 13

Mom and Dad disappeared into The Room to "talk this over."

This time, they closed The Door, so Beck and I couldn't spy on them.

Instead, we went topside with our books to do a little reading. (Reading about the adventures of Poseidon and his Lightning Thief son are even better when you're on the open sea breathing in all that salty air.)

Tommy spent the time working on his hair. He has a whole closet full of product. Gels and stuff. He uses the breeze coming off the sea as his blow-dryer.

Storm killed time memorizing our new boat's bilge pump manual. When she was done with that, she moved on to devouring *Ships' Bilge Pumps: An Illustrated History.*

About an hour later, Mom and Dad emerged from The Room and called a family meeting at the stern of the ship. (That means the rear end. Of the boat.)

"We think we should accept Nathan Collier's challenge," Mom announced.

"Whoo-hoo!" I shouted because I was jazzed. "We'll show those Collier kids who the world's greatest treasure-hunting kids are!"

"Should I turn the boat around and lay in a course for London?" asked Tommy.

"We're almost to Port Said, Egypt," said Storm, calculating the voyage to the United Kingdom in her head. "If we head west and north, take the route through the Strait of Gibraltar, it's three thousand seventy-one miles. At an average speed of ten knots, it'll take twelve, maybe thirteen days. If we decide to head south through the Suez Canal, swing around the Cape of Good Hope at the southern tip of Africa, and then head north, we're talking forty-seven days, give or take an hour or so."

Mom and Dad smiled. "Impressive mental math, Stephanie," said Mom.

Storm beamed. "Thank you. I try."

"But," said Dad, "we're not going to meet Collier in London as he suggested."

"He's agreed to discuss this idea with us in Egypt," added Mom. "UNESCO has already contacted the Egyptian Supreme Council of Antiquities. They'll meet us at the dock in Port Said and happily take possession of the long-lost sarcophagus."

"Collier will arrange a vehicle for us in Port Said," said Dad. "We'll leave *The Lost Again* docked in the port and drive down to the Faiyum Oasis where Collier will be with his children."

"If," said Mom.

Dad nodded. "If you four are up to the challenge. Your mother and I think you should do this. It's time to rewrite the popular narrative. To erase as many of Nathan Collier's untruths as we can. However, the decision is yours."

"It has to be," said Mom. "This contest will be all on you. You'll be on your own. Your father and I won't be able to offer you any assistance or guidance. You'll have to do all your own research. Make your own decisions."

"It'll be Kidds versus kids," said Dad.

"Of course," Mom said proudly, "you four have done your own treasure hunting quite expertly in the past."

We were all nodding and maybe choking up a little bit. The greatest treasures we ever found? Mom and Dad. When they were lost or kidnapped, Tommy, Storm, Beck, and I were the ones who found 'em and brought 'em home!

"So?" said Mom, anticipation twinkling in her eye. "What do you think?"

Tommy stepped forward first.

"Let's do this thing!" he shouted.

"Booyah!" Beck and I hollered together. We pumped our fists to the sky. We also did a little touchdown dance.

Finally, Storm weighed in.

"Indubitably," she said.

We all kind of stared at her.

"Hey," she said, "if that brainy Kioni Collier can use the word, so can I."

The vote was unanimous.

We Kidd kids were ready to take on the Collier kids!

CHAPTER 14

At the dock in Port Said, we posed for a few photos with the Egyptian antiquities people, who were super excited to have the Fourth Dynasty pharaoh's three-ton black basalt stone coffin back in Egypt where it belonged.

While Mom and Dad were shaking hands with all the dignitaries, Beck whispered to me, "How long before Collier takes credit for finding this treasure, too?"

I nodded. And smiled for the cameras. Sure, Beck, Tommy, Storm, and I were in the background for all the pictures, but we still wanted to look good. When we beat the Collier kids in the tournament of treasure hunters, our smiles would be front and center and splashed on the cover of archaeological magazines everywhere! Maybe. You never know. We could always get bumped off the cover by a dinosaur bone find or an interesting pottery shard.

We spent the night in Port Said at the Palma Hotel (yes, there were palm trees around the pool) and, since we were eager to start our four-and-a-half-hour journey south from Port Said to the Faiyum Oasis, we grabbed a quick on-the-run Egyptian street food breakfast sandwich called a ful.

It's made from fava beans mashed into paste. Probably why it stuck to the roof of my mouth. Just meant I could enjoy it longer.

"Remnants of ful were discovered in a number of the Twelfth Dynasty pharaoh tombs from nearly two thousand years BC," Storm advised us as we gobbled down our breakfast sandwiches.

Beck wasn't enjoying her beans and pita as much as I was. "I wonder if these beans are from that same batch."

After breakfast, the six of us piled into the

vehicle that Nathan Collier had delivered to our hotel. And I use the term *vehicle* loosely. *Rattletrap piece of junk* might be a better descriptor.

"It's an old Cairo microbus," said Tommy, who had a thing for cars and, I guess, microbuses. Even grungy ones with ratty seats that looked like a camel had been nibbling on them.

"Granted, it's not much to look at," said Dad, who, by the way, is an eternal optimist. "But to be a microbus on the bustling streets of Cairo, this has to be a hardy vehicle."

"And," said Mom, trying to add her cheery spin, "we have the Faiyum Oasis to look forward to!"

"A beautiful spot," said Storm, as we climbed into the exposed foam seats in the back of the microbus. "A magical lake in the middle of the desert that changes colors depending on the time of day. There are also patches of green, cascading waterfalls, and Whale Valley, which is filled with the fossilized skeletons of whales, sharks, and other sea creatures from forty million years ago when the desert was an ocean."

Tommy cranked the ignition. Our microbus lurched away from the curb. It rattled and clattered and clinked and clanked like a forty-million-year-old whale fossil.

This was going to be a long car ride.

I should've used more deodorant.

CHAPTER 15

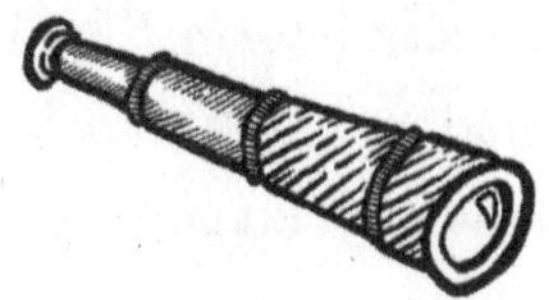

We traveled south on the Ismailia Desert Road.

As you might imagine, since it was a desert road, we saw a lot of sand.

It was tan.

And reddish yellow.

Beige, too.

Then, about five miles north of the oasis, our microbus died. Of course it did.

Maybe it wanted to join all those other ancient whales in that valley.

We had to walk the rest of the way. Because

Collier had given us a broken-down hunk of junk. So, we trudged on.

That's when the wind kicked up.

We were in a sandstorm. The kind that really stings. I clenched my teeth to keep out the big stuff, but I knew my boogers were going to be beige for days.

"Head for that boulder!" shouted Dad over the whine of the swirling wind.

"We'll hunker down there until the brown blizzard blows through!" hollered Mom.

"My hair is a mess!" cried Tommy. The sand stuck to his head like his hairdo was a wadded-up ball of sandpaper. I bet he wished he hadn't used so much hair gel that morning.

We sheltered against that rock for nearly an hour. It was the longest hour of my life. It was like we were stuck inside the bottom half of an hour-glass waiting for all the sand to rain down on top of our heads. When the winds finally died down, I looked up as the sky went from brown to blue.

There was a camera drone hovering overhead. It had an "Adventure Channel" logo slapped on it.

"Collier!" This time when I spat out the *k* sound in the name, the spittle took some lip-sand flying along with it.

I had a feeling the drone had been following us for a while because the broken-down microbus scene and the sandstorm were both going to be part of Nathan Collier's new TV show.

The tournament hadn't even officially started, but we already looked like losers.

CHAPTER 16

Bewildered, windblown, and bedraggled, we hiked the final two miles to the oasis.

We were so coated with sand, we looked like walking sand zombies.

We reached a clump of ancient buildings ringing the Faiyum Oasis, which Storm reminded us wasn't really an oasis because it was fed with water from the Nile River. None of us really cared. We just wanted any kind of water to wash away all the dust we'd collected on our hike.

Unfortunately, we didn't have a change of clothes or any supplies. We'd left all that behind in the broken-down microbus.

We stepped under some shady palm trees.

And Nathan Collier was waiting for us.

With a camera.

"Hello, Nathan," said Dad.

"Hello, Thomas," said Collier, smiling his smarmy smile. "So good of you to accept my invitation."

"Nice of you to meet us here in Egypt instead of London," said Mom.

Her words were polite, but I saw she was giving him The Look. The same one she gave us when we did something we really weren't supposed to do.

"Always happy to oblige a fellow treasure hunter," said Collier, bouncing up on the balls of his feet.

Tommy raised his hand.

"Ah, young Tailspin Tommy!" said Collier. "We meet again."

"I guess we do," said Tommy. "But this time you don't get to do any kind of ancient ritual on me. Incan, Egyptian, any of 'em—especially if they involve knives."

Collier raised his right hand like he was making a solemn vow. "You have my word."

"Ha!" Beck and I both chuffed a laugh. Collier's

word was about as good as his broken-down microbus.

Storm stepped forward. “We, the four Kidd kids, accept your challenge. We will compete against your children—the four not currently in prison—in this treasure-hunting tournament.”

Dad moved in to stand beside Storm. “It’s time we set the record straight, Nathan. Are you seriously claiming that you found Paititi, the Lost City of Gold?”

Collier shrugged and smiled innocently. “If it’s on the internet, if I see a video clip on YouTube, then it has to be true.”

“Unless it’s a lie!” I blurted.

“You tell ’em, Bick!” yelled Beck.

“I just did!”

“I know. I heard you.”

“Cool.”

“Our family’s good name and reputation is seriously harmed every time you make a false claim,” said Dad.

“I’m sorry, Thomas,” said Collier.

Was he apologizing? Nope. Because right after the *I'm sorry* came a big *but.*

"But I believe your family's name was already seriously tarnished all the way back in 1945. The actions of your grandfather, Captain Joseph Kidd, at Königsberg Castle were negligent to say the least."

There it was again. Königsberg Castle. Just like the subject of that thick folder Mom and Dad kept in The Room. How come Collier already knew about it but we didn't? Well, we did, but we had to snoop and eavesdrop to know what we now knew.

"How the heck did you get out of jail, man?" demanded Tommy, totally losing his usual mellow.

I could tell Collier's needling of Dad was really working Tommy's nerves. Plus, Tommy's hair was still a sandblasted mess. Bad grooming always makes Tommy grumpy.

"Well, young Thomas, if you must know, I had excellent lawyers. And my Peruvian partner,

Senor Rojas, knows people who know people. The right kind of people."

"By which," said Storm, "you mean the wrong type of people."

Collier exhaled in loud exasperation. "Look, if you Kidds find me or my invitation objectionable in any way, we can call this whole thing off, right now."

"What's the matter, Nathan?" said Mom. "Afraid your kids will lose?"

A sinister grin curled across Collier's face. "Impossible. Have you met my children?"

When he said that, I heard the WHUMP-WHUMP-WHUMP of an approaching whirlybird.

"Ah, here they come now." Collier shielded his eyes and gazed up at the helicopter swooping in to make a landing.

Only, it wasn't going to land.

It hovered about fifty feet above the desert floor. Kirk, Kioni, Carlos, and Kaiyo jumped out of both sides of the chopper and rappelled to the ground on ropes!

WOW. THEY MADE A MUCH BETTER ENTRANCE THAN WE DID.
YA THINK?

CHAPTER 17

Mom and Dad went into a nearby building with Nathan Collier to work out the details for the upcoming competition.

We waited outside. With the Collier kids.

Us looking like something the camel just dragged in.

Them looking even more amazing than they did on YouTube.

Plus, under their jumping-out-of-a-helicopter fatigues, they had these really awesome matching tracksuits. Kirk, Kioni, Carlos, and Kaiyo looked like they were all set to march into the Olympic stadium for the opening ceremonies, and Kirk would probably be the guy lighting the torch.

"You must be Tommy," said Kirk, sizing up his direct competition. "How much can you bench-press?"

"Three hundred and fifty pounds," Tommy proudly replied. "How about you?"

"A Buick."

"Excuse me?" said Storm.

"Kirk works out with automobiles," said Kaiyo, the snarky one. "Pay attention, chucklehead."

"Whoa," said Tommy. "Storm isn't a chucklehead. She's a genius."

"Is that so?" said Kioni with a confident smirk. "What has a spine but no bones?"

"A book," Storm snapped back.

"What gets wetter and wetter the more it dries?"

"A towel."

"How can a man go eight days without sleep?"

"Easy," said Storm with a smirk of her own. "He sleeps at night."

Kioni begrudgingly nodded. "You're good."

"And you're good looking," said Tommy, giving

So, Kioni, WHERE HAVE YOU BEEN ALL MY LIFE?
HIDING FROM YOU.

his eyebrows a wiggle workout. "How'd you get so beautiful?"

Kaiyo answered for her big sister. "She took your share, uggo."

That startled Tommy. "I'm, uh, having a bad hair day."

"You two are twins?" said Carlos, the twelve-year-old, gesturing toward me and Beck.

"That's right," said Beck.

"Huh. And most people try not to make the same mistake twice."

Fortunately, that's when Mom, Dad, and Mr. Collier came out to brief us.

"We've come to terms," Dad announced.

"This will be a best two-out-of-three competition," added Mom.

"We will test your skills in a series of simulated treasure hunts," said Collier. "The contest will be recorded for broadcast purposes and is being sponsored by the Polish video game company Pleyon and its billionaire owner, Mertin Schmerkel, the richest man in all of Poland."

"Pleyon games are good," said Tommy.

"I like their slogan," said Kirk.

Tommy nodded. "Totally."

They chanted the game maker's slogan together: "Play on with Pleyon. Play! On!"

Then they both giggled. I had the sense that, if we weren't at war with the Colliers, Tommy and Kirk might've become buds. They might've even bench-pressed automobiles together.

"We were happy to learn that the treasure quest challenges," Mom continued, "will be scripted by a very eminent archaeologist, Dr. Hieronymus Whittley."

"We know him," said Dad. "In fact, he was a professor of mine in college."

"I read the SparkNotes study guide for one of his lectures," said Collier proudly. "Well, I skimmed it."

"For the first treasure hunt," said Dad, "we've been told that Professor Whittley has created clues for two separate paths to the same object."

"We don't want you buffoons following us," quipped Kaiyo.

"This is all fake?" said Storm. "Fictitious?

We're used to hunting real treasures."

"As are we," said Kioni.

"Riiiiight," said Storm. "Loved seeing you at the Lost City of Gold with all the wee, little people."

"Chya," laughed Tommy. "That was our diorama from the Smithsonian exhibit."

"Look, Kidds," said Collier, "think of this tournament as a series of treasure-hunting *games*. The challenges will be real even if the treasures you find are somewhat bogus." He looked pointedly at Dad. "It might also be a way for you to, how shall I put this, rehabilitate the Kidd family name."

The hair was bristling on the back of my neck. Beck's was, too. It's another twin thing—an annoyed twin thing.

"We're the Kidds," I said. "We're the best treasure-hunting family the world has ever known!"

"Hang on, hot dog," said Kaiyo, the snotty little totty. "For that to be true, you have to beat us. Good luck with that. You don't have a snowball's chance at the center of the earth."

“The temperature at the earth’s core is nine thousand three hundred and ninety-two degrees Fahrenheit,” said Kioni. “Do you need that in Celsius?”

“No, thanks,” said Storm, tapping the side of her head. “Already got it.”

We’d all heard enough.

The four of us stepped forward and shook hands with our four opponents.

“Game on,” said Tommy. “Game on!”

PART TWO
GAME ON!

CHAPTER 18

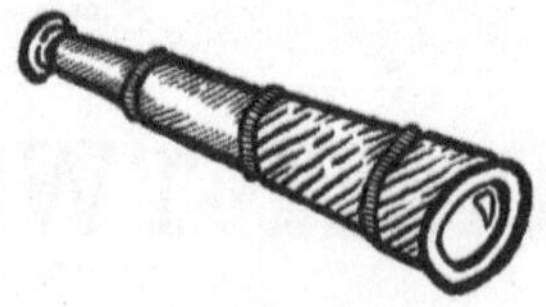

The next day, Nathan Collier's crew delivered us to a nearby airstrip and a very swanky private jet—proving that he was still very wealthy and could've sent a stretch limo to pick us up instead of that rattletrap clunker.

He just wanted us to make that sandblasted entrance so his kids would look even better than they already did.

"Mertin Schmerkel paid for it," explained Carlos, when he heard me whistle with disbelief the instant we set foot inside the posh plane's cabin. "Schmerkel's paying for everything. When you're a bazillionaire, you can do that sort of thing."

Carlos strutted up the aisle and plunked down in the window seat I would've taken if I wasn't so busy gawking at my surroundings.

Instead of ordinary plane seats where your knees dig into the back of the person in front of you, we each had our own puffy, swivel-able leather recliner. The wood paneling on the bulkheads was made out of real wood, not plastic. There were all sorts of sandwiches and snacks and soda pop in the galley plus a flight attendant to bring them to us.

I could tell: Schmerkel was spending big bucks to produce this *World's Greatest Treasure-Hunting Kids!* show. He probably had a deal with Netflix.

Mom and Dad didn't join us on the flight. Neither did Nathan Collier. It was just me, Beck, Storm, and Tommy with Kirk, Kioni, Carlos, and Kaiyo. The only grown-up flying with us was a line producer named Bailey Bigelow. She was our show runner. I guess that meant she would run the show. Either that, or she'd be training for a marathon when the cameras weren't rolling.

"The rest of the production crew will meet us when we land in England," said Bailey. "Actually, it's two crews. Hair, makeup, lights, sound, camera. One for each team."

"You say we're flying to England?" said Storm.

"England is a country that is part of the United Kingdom," blurted Kioni. "It shares land borders with Wales to the west and Scotland to the north."

Yep. The brainy Collier kid could do a Wiki-brain-dump as fast as Storm.

Storm rolled her eyes. "More third-grade-geography-report-level information," she muttered before continuing her question. "If I may, in what part of England will be visiting?"

"Lincolnshire," said Bailey.

"Which was named after Abraham Lincoln!" shouted Tommy like he was a contestant on a TV quiz show. He shot a wink to Kioni. I think he was trying to impress her with his brains as well as his bod. He should've stuck to his strong suit.

Not that Tommy needs to wear a suit for his bod to look strong. Those muscles are for reals.

"Um, Tommy?" I whispered. "I don't think Abraham Lincoln was even born back in the olden days when English people started naming cities and shires and stuff."

"Chya," said Tommy, faking a chuckle. "Everybody knows that, Bick. I was just busting your chops, bro." He shot Kioni another wink. She rolled her eyes.

The jet took off. Bailey didn't give us any more details or specifics about our first treasure quest. Just that it would be "exciting, thrilling, and extremely challenging."

"Will there be any opportunities for horseback riding?" asked Storm, who's the best rider in our family. (She and her trusty steed chased down a bad guy in our last adventure. It was awesome.) "Lincolnshire has a rich equestrian history," Storm continued. "And the Wolds, the highest point in the area, is the perfect setting for riding."

"We don't do horses," said Kaiyo, the snarky

one. "Too stinky. Too much poop. We prefer motorcycles and ATVs."

"We do those, too!" snapped Beck.

"Totally!" I said. "We have mad skills on dirt bikes."

"Yeah," cracked Carlos. "I hear you both got a nine out of ten on your last driver's tests because one guy was able to jump out of the way."

"You know the most dangerous part of a dirt bike?" sniped Kaiyo. "The nut that connects the seat to the handlebars."

Tommy got that puzzled, wrinkled-brow look he sometimes gets when he's confused. "There's a nut that does that?"

"Yeah," said Kaiyo. "You!"

She and Carlos slapped each other an across-airplane-aisle high five. Kioni chuckled. Kirk did a backward donkey-honk laugh.

"Let's save it for the competition, huh, kids?" said Bailey. And for those of you listening to this being read aloud, when she said *kids*, she wasn't just talking to us.

“Bailey is correct, my brother and sisters,” said Kirk. “Let us be chill.”

The more I listened to Kirk Collier, the more I heard some kind of stiff Austrian accent. Like Ah-nold, the guy from the Terminator movies.

“Focus on what is important,” said Kirk. “We might be airborne, but we need to stick to our content production schedule.”

“Yes, Kirk, whatever you say, Kirk,” said Kaiyo sarcastically.

But she and the other Colliers dutifully pulled out their phones and started filming selfie videos.

“We’re all social media influencers,” explained Carlos when he saw us gawping at him as he moved through a series of weird hand gestures and goofy poses. “Everything I’m wearing is hashtagged, baby. We’re what they call a revenue stream.”

“We make it rain money!” added Kaiyo.

I started wondering if I could be an Instagram or TikTok influencer, too.

Storm shook her head. I could tell she was

BICK INFLUENCING ME TO HURL.

disgusted by the Collier kids. "What kind of treasure hunters are you people?"

"Easy," said Kirk, striking some more bodybuilder poses for his phone. "The kind that bring the treasure home, twenty-four seven."

"We are all currently pursuing money-making opportunities," said Kioni, smiling into her phone. "Therefore, we are actively hunting treasure."

Yep. The Colliers spent the whole flight filming videos to post on their various social media channels. Me? I had better things to do with my time.

Specifically, I needed to take a nap. So did Tommy, Storm, and Beck.

A few hours and a puddle of pillow drool later, we were all awoken by the same soft ding of a bell.

The one that meant our private jet was about to land near Lincolnshire, England.

I'm sure some part of Tommy was hoping that Abe would be there in his stovepipe hat to greet us.

CHAPTER 19

The jet touched down at a private airfield outside Lincolnshire, England.

Honest Abe was nowhere to be seen, except on a crinkled five-dollar bill I had stuffed in my pocket.

We piled into an SUV. The Colliers piled into their own identical SUV. Bailey Bigelow climbed into one of several production vans. Our convoy was heading toward the east coast of England.

"They call this East Anglia," said Storm, not that anybody asked her. "It's where Norfolk meets Lincolnshire."

"Norfolk?" said Tommy, giving us another one of his confused looks. This one was more of a puppy-dog head tilt. "How'd we wind up in Virginia?"

Storm very gently explained how the Norfolk in Virginia was named after the one in England.

Tommy nodded. "Huh. Guess that makes naming things easier."

Our SUV pulled into a grassy field dotted with tiny yellow weed flowers.

"That's the Cross Keys Bridge," said Storm, pointing to an impressive cast-iron structure. I noticed a small construction site on the far bank. I figured it was for some kind of repairs.

"It's a swing bridge," Storm continued. "It swings to the side to let vessels pass. It spans the tidal River Nene. When the North Sea tide rises, that shallow, brown water will flow upstream as fast as a human sprinter. During a full moon, the water can move faster than a galloping horse."

"Cool," said Tommy.

"Not for Bad King John."

"The guy from the Robin Hood stories?" I said.

Storm nodded. "In 1216, when King John and his army were fleeing from their enemies, they tried to cross the mudscape of this tidal estuary known as the Wash."

"What's an estuary?" asked Tommy.

"The mouth of a large river, where the ocean tide meets the freshwater stream," I said, because I (unlike, apparently, Tommy) had been paying attention that day in boat-home school.

"Correct," said Storm.

"Give yourself a gold star, Bick," said Beck. "Do you also know what the Wash is? Because you don't seem to do it very often. With your body or your clothes."

I ignored her. It gets easier with time. Trust me. "So, what happened when Bad King John tried to cross through the mud?" I asked Storm.

"The rapidly rising waters caught his baggage train. The wheels of his wagons did not go round and round. They became mired in quicksand. Horses panicked and bolted. Treasure chests and trunks were swept away by the swift current. All of the kingdom's treasure was lost—including King John's crown jewels!"

That got our juices and our imaginations

flowing. The Collier kids might be all about the treasure you can take to the bank. We Kidds loved the kind that belonged in history museums!

Tommy snapped his fingers. "Of course. This is our first treasure quest in the competition. We have to find King John's crown jewels."

"Or," said Storm, "the cheap imitation version of them."

Storm was right. This was going to be a staged treasure hunt. More like an Easter egg hunt in your neighbor's backyard than the real deal. Somebody had scripted the whole thing. Still, the thrill of the hunt would be exciting. Like Mom says, sometimes the journey is more important than the destination. And sometimes the quest is more important than the actual treasure.

I was pumped.

But, I could tell Storm was still feeling grumpy about the pretend nature of this whole thing.

"Our adventures for this TV show are going to be like a series of trips to an escape room in a strip mall."

"Doesn't matter, sis," said Tommy. "The treasure may be fake but the quest is always real."

He sounded a little like a coach. Or a motivational meme. One of those.

Professor Hieronymus Whittley, Dad's old archaeology professor, was waiting for us and the Colliers on the banks of the estuary. And by old, I mean ancient. Professor Whittley had to be ninety-some years old. He had more hair growing out of his ears than his head.

"Dude," said Kaiyo, "you're so old, you probably have hieroglyphics on your driver's license."

"Yeah," said Carlos, "you're so old, when you were a kid, rainbows were just in black and white."

They slapped each other another high five.

"You are indeed advanced in your years," said Kioni.

"Sir, do you burp dust?" asked Kirk. (I think he was being sincere.)

None of us Kidds made any wisecracks. Well, at least not out loud. That would have been rude. But I was thinking that when Moses parted the Red Sea, Professor Whittley might've been on the other side fishing.

"You are quite right, you cheeky little whippersnappers," the professor said in a creaky, squeaky voice. With his British accent, he sounded like an antique butler. "I am indeed old. Ninety-five, to be precise."

The professor turned to look at Tommy, Storm, Beck, and me with his milky blue eyes.

“The same age your great-grandfather Jumpin’ Joe Kidd would’ve been if he were still with us.”

“Did you know our father’s grandfather?” I asked.

“Too right,” said the professor. “I knew him. He looked like you back in the day.” He jabbed a wrinkled finger in Tommy’s general direction. “I also knew all about the foolish and barmy thing he did.”

“What was it?” asked Tommy eagerly.

The professor’s face went blank. Apparently, so did his brain.

“I don’t recall. However, the thing he did? It was foolish. And barmy. I remember that much. Disastrous, too!”

Oh-kay. So much for getting the Kidd family 411 from Dad’s old archaeology professor.

“So why are we here, professor?” asked Kioni Collier.

“To find King John’s lost treasure,” said Storm, “or a reasonable facsimile thereof. Correct?”

The old professor smiled. “Well played, young lady. Well played, indeed. You are correct.”

Storm smirked at Kioni and marked an imaginary one in the air to show that she'd just scored first.

Kioni smirked back. "I prefer to tally points after the victory is complete. Not before the game has even started."

And then the two brainiacs glared at each other.

"Right-oh. Enough glaring!" cried Professor Whittley. "Children? It is time for your first clue packet!"

CHAPTER 20

"Roll all cameras!" shouted Logan Bigelow, the director of the TV show. "Scene one, quest one, take one!"

A guy with horn-rimmed glasses handed index cards to Kirk and Tommy.

"I'm George," he said. "Harvard grad. Head writer. Memorize your lines. Fast!"

Tommy and Kirk scanned the cards with fast-flying eyeballs. They were doing a one-hundred-character reading dash. They both had very intense competitive streaks.

"Got it," said Kirk, beating Tommy's "Got it" by half a second.

"And action!" cried Logan.

"Welcome to *The World's Greatest Treasure-Hunting Kids!*" said Kirk.

"Brought to you by the game-making wizards at Pleyon!" said Tommy.

Then they both chanted, "Play on. With Pleyon!" They also both clapped their hands together twice. I guess that's how the Pleyon jingle goes. (I know it's how you clap on and clap off your lights with the Clapper.)

Professor Hieronymus Whittley tottered into the scene. In his tweed jacket and vest, he looked like he'd just stepped out of an Indiana Jones movie.

"And so, the competition begins."

When the lights were on and the cameras were rolling, the old guy didn't sound nearly as frail and shaky as he had earlier.

"The Collier kids versus the Kidd kids for the title of..."

He held a beat. I figured they were going to add some dramatic DUN-DUN-DUN music later.

"...The World's Greatest Treasure-Hunting Kids!"

"That's us!" blurted Tommy. "We're the Kidds!"

"Ah," said the professor, raising one gnarly finger. "But are you Kidds the greatest treasure-hunting kids? We'll soon find out. I have in my suitcoat pocket two envelopes."

He slid them out dramatically.

"One clue for each team. You will both be pursuing the same goal: find and retrieve Bad King John's crown jewels, part of the treasure lost somewhere on the banks of the River Nene. Your clues will take you on separate paths, different but equally arduous journeys. In the end, both routes will lead to and converge at the same destination. The crown. The treasure. The victory!"

Whoa. The old guy was good. The professor gave a total PBS-quality delivery. He even had that very proper English accent, which I guess wasn't really that big of deal. After all, we were in England.

Professor Whittley handed one envelope to Kirk. One to Tommy. It was very dramatic.

"Play on," said the professor.

"With Pleyon!" shouted Tommy and Kirk.

Tommy hustled over to where the rest of us Kidds were clustered. Kirk dashed off to huddle with his siblings. Lights, boom microphones, and cameras followed both teams' every move. The Colliers were used to all the Hollywood stuff. We weren't. But after knocking over a few light stands, bumping into the sound dude (twice), and sending a camera operator flying backward into a mud puddle, we got used to it pretty quickly and, more or less, forgot they were even there.

"Tear open the envelope!" Beck urged Tommy.

"Chya!" Tommy flipped open his Swiss Army knife blade and used it like a crocodile hunter's letter opener. It made for way better TV than just slicing through the envelope's thin paper with the tip of his fingernail.

"Hurry, Tommy," coached Beck. "The Colliers are already reading their clue card."

"This way!" we heard Kioni shout. "I know where the clue is taking us!"

The Colliers trotted off to the cast-iron bridge following their brainy sister.

"Tommy?" said Beck. "They're getting a head start."

"What's the clue say?" I asked.

"Here, Bick," said Tommy, handing me the bright-red card he'd just pulled out of the envelope. His hands were trembling slightly. "You're the family wordsmith. Read these words."

"The Colliers are running across the bridge!" reported Beck. "Hurry, Bick. What's our clue?"

I focused on the card and read what it said: "In a day filled with mud and grief, this would have given the bad king some welcome relief."

Storm exhaled one of her gustier sighs. I could tell. She didn't like rhyming clues. Or red clue cards. Or anything about this make-believe treasure hunt at all.

"The clue is a rhyme?" she fumed. "This is exactly like one of those silly escape room games!"

"Totally," said Tommy. "And guess what, Storm? We're gonna win it!"

"Because we have to!" I added.

"Our family reputation is on the line!" shouted Beck.

"Not to mention that whole thing about Dad's grandpa," I said.

"Yeah," said Tommy, "what's up with that?"

Of course, that's when we heard Kaiyo Collier scream from the middle of the bridge. "Here it is! Upstairs. Our second clue!" Then she whistled. Very loudly. A cafeteria-quieting whistle. "Hey, Kidds, guess what?" she hollered. "We're gonna crush you!"

CHAPTER 21

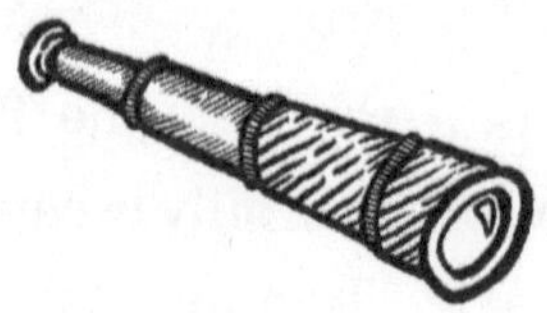

"You guys?" said Beck. "We're wasting too much time! What's up with our clue?"

"I don't know," I hollered at her.

"Well, neither do I," Beck hollered back.

"Guess it's another twin thing," I screamed.

"I guess!" She screamed it louder. Also her face was turning red. Fine. She says my face was purple. (She'd show you but she only does black-and-white sketches when we're in the middle of a mission.)

"Tommy?" said Storm, who must've been thinking the whole time Beck and I were screaming.

"Flip out the magnifying glass on your Swiss Army knife."

"No problemo," said Tommy, fidgeting with all the blades, tweezers, and screwdrivers on his multifunction device. He levered the tiny magnifying glass into place.

Now Storm turned to me. "Bick? Roll that clue card up into a tube—as wide as the lens on Tommy's magnifying glass."

I did as I was told. Meanwhile. Storm was flicking open the magnifying glass on *her* Swiss Army knife. (They're standard Kidd Family Treasure Hunter gear. Dad has the Wenger Giant model: 141 functions on 87 folding tools. The thing is nine inches wide and weighs two pounds. It's a real pocket sagger!)

Storm lined up her magnifying glass with the near end of the cardboard tube. Tommy held his up against the far end. Our brilliant sister had built herself a tiny telescope and was checking out something on the far side of the bridge.

"You guys?" she said, sounding excited. "There's a Porty John over there at that construction site."

Seriously? I thought. *That's her big discovery?* Good thing Storm was never up in the crow's nest of some explorer's ship shouting, *Avast! Chemical toilet, ho!*

"This isn't the best time for a bathroom break, Storm!" said Beck.

"I know that, Rebecca," Storm replied. "But we are in England. Here in the UK, a portable toilet is called a Portaloo, not a Porta-Potty or Porty John. In fact, Portaloo is a British and European Community registered trademark."

"So, why is that one over there a Porty John, like in the United States?" wondered Tommy. He even stroked his lantern jaw while he was doing the wondering.

"Because of Bad King *John*," said Storm, who all of a sudden didn't seem to mind rhyming clues because she'd just figured one out. "It's part of the cutesy-poo clue. The portable toilet would've given him 'welcome relief.'"

"Chya," said Tommy. "He could've relieved himself over there."

"He also could've grossed himself out," added

Beck. "Those things always stink. And nobody ever flushes."

"Because they're non-flushable toilets," said Storm. "You see, a chemical toilet operates—"

"You guys?" I said. "We don't have time for a chemistry lesson. We need to be on the other side of that bridge! Right now. Our clue is in that toilet!"

Okay. That sounded bad. But it was true. Our clue card was sending us to a construction site on the far side of the murky River Nene.

We took off running. As we crossed the bridge, I looked up at the gazebolike structure perched on top of its cast-iron arches and trusses. The Colliers were inside what had to be the swing bridge's control house. The place where you could make the whole bridge pivot sideways to allow ships to pass.

And one of the Collier kids was flipping those switches. My guess? Brainy Kioni. She probably had a PhD in structural engineering and could build a science project suspension bridge out of yarn, dry spaghetti strands, and toothpicks.

When we hit the midpoint of the bridge, the whole A17 highway started sliding slowly to the left.

"We need to be in that toilet!" cried Tommy, leading the charge.

We reached the far end of the bridge just as it slipped free from the edge of the roadway.

"Jump!" I shouted.

And we all did. Logan and our entire camera crew leapt after us. Hopefully, our billionaire corporate sponsor was giving them hazardous-duty pay.

WOW. THOSE BLOKES MUST REALLY NEED TO USE THE POTTY.
PORTY JOHN

CHAPTER 22

When we reached the Porty John, the little red disk in the doorknob told us it was occupied.

I rapped politely on the plastic door.

"Um, excuse me?" I said.

"Wait yer turn, mate," came the gruff reply.

"This is, uh, sort of an emergency."

"Ask me if I bloody care."

"No, thank you." I retreated two steps.

"I am not treasure hunting in there," whispered Beck, gesturing at the stinky portable toilet.

"We have to," Tommy whispered back.

"It's where the clue is sending us," added Storm.

The plastic door swung open. A burly worker strode out.

"I used the last of the bog roll," he said, gesturing over his shoulder with his thumb.

"Thanks," I said with a smile. "Good to know."

And then the four of us stood there. Staring at the open door. The toilet.

"What are we waiting for?" asked Tommy.

"A gentle breeze?" I suggested.

"You guys?" said Tommy. "The Collier kids are gonna win this round unless one of us goes in there and finds our next clue."

We all nodded.

"Brave of you to volunteer, Tommy," I said.

"Yeah," he said. "I just wish I'd brought my dive mask and a fresh oxygen tank."

Tommy sucked in a deep breath, pinched his nose, and ducked into the Porty John. He slammed the door shut. The rest of us (and the film crew) took another giant step backward.

The molded plastic booth rocked a little as Tommy thrashed around inside it.

Suddenly, the door flew open.

Tommy stumbled out.

He was holding his breath and a small metal box.

"Got it!" he gasped.

"Where was it?" asked Beck.

"You don't want to know. And I'm trying to forget. Luckily, it was wrapped in plastic. Plus, they have a big jug of hand sanitizer in there."

Tommy dropped the tin box on the ground. We all bent down to examine it. There was a latch beneath a four-digit combination lock.

"Our next clue is inside that thing," I said, stating the obvious, which is what I do best.

"We need the combination!" said Beck, stating the next obvious thing.

"Did you see any kind of numerical clue inside the Porty John?" Storm asked Tommy.

He shook his head. "None. Unless you mean number one or number two."

Storm shook her head. "There are four dials of digits. Each with the numbers zero through nine. That means there are ten thousand possible combinations."

"You want to start with one-two-three-four?" said Tommy. "That's my favorite password."

"No," said Storm. "The answer is most likely

linked in some way to our treasure hunt. Our quest for Bad King John's crown jewels."

And that's when the fifty-billion-watt light bulb clicked on in Storm's ginormous brain.

"Of course," she said. "It's 1216. The year the bad king was here. The year he lost all his treasure in the tidal surge as he crossed the muddy river!"

Tommy did the honors. He spun the combination dial to 1-2-1-6.

The latch snapped open. He popped up the metal lid.

Inside the box was a pirate map done up on crinkled parchment paper. There was a big X marking a spot back on the other side of the bridge.

Unfortunately, the bridge was locked in its wide-open position, its span running parallel to the riverbanks.

"We need to swim across!" I said.

"No, we don't," said Beck.

"Yes, we do!"

She shook her head. "Waste of time." She pointed across the river. To where the Collier kids were doing a little jig. An end-zone victory dance.

Because they'd already dug up Bad King John's bejeweled crown. Well, at least the one the prop department had buried on the bank of the River Nene for a team of treasure-hunting kids to dig up.

"How'd they'd get back across the river with the bridge open?" I asked.

On the other side of the stream, Carlos slapped

Kirk on the back. All sorts of water sprayed out of the muscleman's shirt.

"I think *they* swam," said Tommy.

Kioni's smile widened when she saw us staring at her. She licked her finger and marked an invisible one in the air. As promised, she started keeping score when it really counted.

And at the end of round one, the Colliers were ahead of us Kidds. One–zip.

"You guys?" said Tommy, who'd just found some kind of sliding panel inside the lid of the metal box. "There's something else in here."

CHAPTER 23

Since we'd already lost the first round of the competition and had to wait for the swinging bridge to grind its way back into place before we could return to the other side, we focused on the metal box's secret compartment.

"What's in there?" asked Beck.

"An envelope!" replied Tommy.

"What's inside the envelope?" I asked, rolling my hand to suggest to Tommy that we speed things up a little.

Tommy slipped it out.

"An old photograph," he reported. "Two soldier dudes shaking hands over a pile of bombs."

Storm leaned in. "Judging from the uniforms

and their insignia, those two are American and Russian aviators from World War II. People sometimes forgot that the United States and the Soviet Union were allies in that global conflict. It's hard to believe today, but back then, the two countries were united in a common cause: defeating Adolf Hitler."

"Must be why Hitler's name is written on the bombs," said Tommy.

"Yes," said Storm. "In English and Russian Cyrillic letters."

THE ENEMY OF MY ENEMY IS MY FRIEND.

WE BOTH HATE THE SAME PEOPLE.

"There's something on the back of the photo!" I said, because I was the first to see the typewritten note taped to its flip side.

Tommy turned the picture over and read what was on the thin slip of paper.

"Bad King John lost precious jewels in his war. In World War II, your great-grandfather lost something worth even more."

"More rhymes?" said Storm. "Who writes this stuff?"

"George," said everybody on our camera crew.

"He went to Harvard," added Logan Bigelow, the director. "They like poetry at Harvard."

"But why is our great-grandfather getting dragged into this?" I said.

The camera crew members shrugged. They had no idea. Neither did we.

"Hang on to the photo, Tommy," suggested Beck. "It might become important in round two."

"Or three," I said.

"Yeah," said Beck. "If we make it that far." She gestured at the Collier kids celebrating on the other bank of the river. Kirk had just passed the glittering fake crown to Kioni. "They're up by one. Don't forget, this is a best two-out-of-three competition. All the Collier kids need to win is one more victory."

Storm nodded. "I concur with Beck's math."

"Then I do, too," said Tommy.

"You guys?" I said, trying to rally my troops. "We still have a fighting chance. Hey, if you were down three games to none in the World Series but still had four more games to play, would you quit?"

"I don't think they let you do that in baseball," said Tommy. "I mean, they've probably sold a whole bunch of tickets and ordered a ton of hot dogs."

"Plus," I said, "the team that was down by three could still win. They just have to sweep the next four games!"

"Actually," said Storm, "in the entire history of Major League Baseball, the NBA, and the NHL—all of whom have playoff series that can reach a seventh game—teams that were down three–nothing in a series have only come back to win five times. Four times in hockey. Once in baseball."

"Wow," said Tommy. "Is that true?"

Storm shrugged. "Those are the facts. Comebacks like the one we need to accomplish are very rare."

"Well," I said, "good thing this isn't hockey or baseball! This is treasure hunting. We only need two more wins, not four! We just have to give the next two rounds everything we've got."

Tommy, Beck, and Storm all nodded grimly. There was a renewed look of steely determination in their eyes.

"Bick is right," said Beck (not something she admits on a regular basis). "We need to make it to the final round." She pointed at the World War II photograph Tommy was holding. "If only to find out what's up with that clue about Dad's grandpa!"

She was right.

Why did the Colliers' TV people write that hidden compartment clue into our script?

What did Dad's Grandpa Joe have to do with finding the World's Greatest Treasure-Hunting Kids?

There was only one way to find out.

We had to play on!

CHAPTER 24

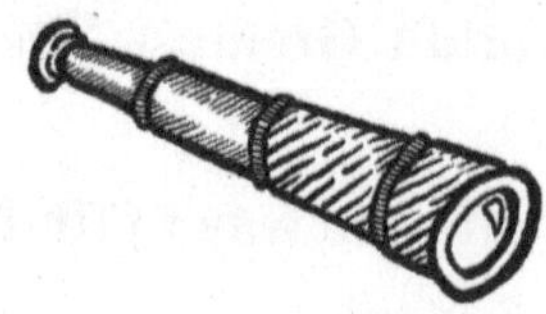

When we were all back on board Nathan Collier's private jet, little Kaiyo made a big show out of stowing Bad King John's "crown" in the overhead luggage bin.

"Oh," she moaned. "It's so heavy. There are so many jewels in it. Kirk? Can you lift it? I think it weighs more than that Buick you bench-press."

"Need a hand, bro?" offered Tommy, because he's sweet that way.

"No, thanks," said Kirk. "It really only weighs about as much as a Whopper at Burger King."

"Because," said Storm, "it is a cheap, imitation,

Hollywood prop. They probably used a glue gun to paste on shattered glass marbles for the phony jewels."

"You're just a sore loser," said Kioni. "One who complains or blames others for their loss."

"I know the etymology of the expression," said Storm.

"Who said anything about studying insects?" countered Kioni.

"That's *entomology*, not etymology," said Storm, eyeing Kioni somewhat suspiciously.

Kioni gave Storm a little stink face. "I know that..."

"Hey, Storm, ease up," said Tommy, leaping to Kioni's defense because he'd fallen in love. Again. "You know what Mom says. If you can't say anything nice, don't say anything at all."

"Fine." Storm crossed her arms over her chest in a huff.

So did Beck and I. Kioni, Carlos, and Kaiyo Collier mirrored our moves.

And things got really, really quiet on board the plane.

WE HAVE TO WIN THIS STARING CONTEST!
FIRST ONE TO BLINK LOSES.
UNLESS A GNAT FLIES INTO THEIR EYE.
WELL, DUH. EVERYBODY KNOWS THE STARING-CONTEST-GNAT-EXCEPTION RULE.
EXIT

The Collier kids sat stewing on their side. We sat fuming on ours. Tommy and Kirk were the only two not majorly mad at the world. They were both playing video games on their phones. Finally, about an hour after takeoff, when the seat belt sign was turned off and we were free to move about the cabin, Bailey Bigelow, the producer, took center stage in the center aisle.

"Okay, kids," she said. "Round one is in the can."

"So is Kirk," said Carlos, gesturing to the restroom at the rear of the plane.

Its door swung open. Kirk came out.

"What'd I miss?" he asked.

"Nothing," said Bailey. "I was just about to brief you all on the second treasure quest in our competition."

"Great," said Beck, as Kirk made his way to his seat. "What fake item will be hunting for this time?"

Bailey smiled, batted her eyes a few times, and pretended like she hadn't heard Beck. I couldn't blame her. I do it sometimes, too. Fine, Beck says she doesn't have to pretend. She never listens to a word I say.

"It's the quest," Tommy whispered through clenched teeth to Beck. "Not the treasure."

I nodded. "We're playing for the Kidd family name. Grandpa Joe. That weird World War II photo."

Now all the Colliers were staring at me. I guess I sounded like I was babbling.

Fortunately, Bailey started talking again. She told us we were headed for the Regionalflugplatz Güttin airport.

Tommy raised his hand. "Is that in Germany?" he asked. "Because those sounded like German words."

"Yes, Thomas. We will be landing at the only airfield on the German Baltic Sea island of Rügen."

Tommy slapped his hands together in triumph. "I knew it sounded German-ish!"

Kaiyo snorted a laugh and turned to Carlos. "That guy Tommy is so dumb, he'd climb over a glass wall just to see what was on the other side."

"Yeah?" I said. "Well, you two are so dumb, when you heard the Baltic Sea was chilly this time of year, you both grabbed a bowl and a spoon."

"You're both so dumb," said Beck, because we're twins and can double-team our opponents, "you talk into an envelope to leave voice mail!"

"Oh, yeah?" said Carlos.

But before he could "so-dumb" us, Kirk and Tommy stood up.

"Enough!" they both said simultaneously.

"Let Bailey finish," said Kirk.

"And then—let's play on," added Tommy.

Then they both chanted, "Play on. With Pleyon." They also clapped their hands together. Twice.

As he was sitting back down, Tommy leaned in to whisper something to Beck, Storm, and me.

"We're doing this for Dad's Grandpa Joe," he reminded us. "Grandpa Joe, Grandpa Joe, Grandpa Joe!"

We all nodded. We would stay focused and

keep our eyes on the prize, even if it was a fake one, because whatever it was, it wasn't the real treasure we were hunting for.

"Are you children familiar with the tenth-century Danish ruler King Harald Blåtand?" asked Bailey.

We all turned to Storm; the Colliers all turned to Kioni.

Storm blurted first.

"He was one of the first kings of Denmark and Norway," she said.

"He died in 986," said Kioni.

Storm went again. "He was known as Bluetooth."

"Because," said Kioni, "he had one discolored tooth."

The factoids kept pinging and ponging across the aisle.

"He had excellent networking and communication skills," said Storm.

"Which is why," added Kioni, "Bluetooth technology is named after him."

Storm served up the topper. "In fact, the

modern Bluetooth logo is made from the Viking rune symbols for *H* and *B* as in Harald Blåtand."

She totally won that battle of the brainiacs when she held up her sketch of the runes and logo on a napkin for everybody to see.

"Very good," said Bailey. "But, did you know that over a thousand years ago Bluetooth, one of the last Viking kings of what is now Denmark, Germany, Sweden, and parts of Norway, left behind a stunning treasure trove of silver coins, pearls, and even a Thor hammer somewhere on the island of Rügen?"

"A Thor hammer," said Tommy. "Kewl!"

Yes, suddenly he was interested in more than redeeming our family name.

Tommy wanted that hammer!

CHAPTER 25

Once again, we left the airport in separate SUVs.

Our driver was part of the production crew. I noticed he was wearing noise-canceling earbuds. Guess he didn't really want to eavesdrop on our conversation. Either that or noisy kids in cars just bugged him.

"Okay, you guys," I said when we were underway. "This is our must-win round. If we lose, the competition is over."

"We know, Bick," said Beck. "We can count."

I turned to Storm. "What can you tell us about

King Bluetooth's treasure?" I asked, bracing myself for the info dump.

Storm did not disappoint.

"Mom and Dad had this fabled treasure island on their list in The Room."

"Yes!" I said, giving that news a hearty arm pump. If it was on The List in The Room, that meant it was a major-league treasure worth finding.

"Bailey gave a partial list of what was buried on the island of Rügen," Storm continued.

"I call dibs on the Thor hammer!" said Tommy.

Storm ignored him. "There were also braided-silver collars, finger rings, and over six hundred rare coins from ancient Saxon, Ottoman, Danish, and Byzantine kingdoms."

"We're gonna need a bigger piggy bank!" I joked.

"Perhaps," said Storm, who didn't sound very excited about all the treasure. "King Harald Blåtand reigned from 958 to 986, but the oldest coin he buried, a Damascus dirham, dates to the year 714."

"Wait a second," said Beck. "How can you know all these gritty details?"

"Easy," said Storm. "All the buried treasure has already been dug up."

"Somebody else scored the Thor hammer?" said Tommy, sounding sad.

Storm nodded. "Did any of you notice when Mom and Dad took the Viking king's buried treasure off their list in The Room?"

We all shook our heads.

"Well," said Storm. "I did."

She tapped her temple. It was just another file in her stockpile of photographic memories.

"It was found a few years ago. A thirteen-year-old German boy named Luca and his math teacher were on the island using metal detectors. Luca pinged the first coin in an open field. They alerted the archaeological authorities."

We all nodded. We knew the rules of the treasure-hunting game.

"Everything was kept hush-hush so they could plan a proper, professional dig."

"Well," I said, "I sure hope that kid with the metal detector got to keep a few of the coins..."

"So, there's nothing left for us to find?" said Beck.

"Oh, I'm sure the TV people will bury something," said Storm. "Maybe even a Thor hammer."

"I hope it's the one from the Avengers movies," said Tommy. "That would be so awesome."

"I hope we find something else," I said.

"What?" said Beck. "You want Thor's red cape?"

"Nope. I want to know what's up with that

photograph of Great-Grandpa Joe from World War II."

"Hey, Storm?" said Beck.

"Yes, Rebecca?"

"You said the kid was out here treasure hunting with his math teacher?"

Storm smiled. "Very good, Rebecca. You show a keen attention for details."

Beck shrugged. "I'm an artist. It's what we do."

(True. Even if those details are often wrong. For instance, stink lines. How can they come out of my ears?)

"This particular math teacher," said Storm, "was also something of a genius."

"Takes one to know one," said Tommy with a wink.

Storm actually blushed a beat before she told us the rest of her story. "He cracked a thousand-year-old secret code that had been baffling treasure hunters for centuries. It gave the precise coordinates of the Viking king's buried booty."

"No way," said Tommy. "The guy actually used math?"

Storm raised both eyebrows. "A lot of people do, Tommy. Every day."

Tommy nodded thoughtfully. "Good to know."

"The secret code led to a field near the village of Schaprode here on the island."

"Do you think that same field is where the TV people will bury our imitation treasure?" I whispered to Storm because I didn't want the Colliers to hear me say it, even though they were at least three car lengths behind us inside their own SUV.

Hey, we couldn't be too careful. The Colliers were super talented. Who knows—Carlos or Kaiyo might've been lip-readers.

"It's definitely one possibility," said Storm. "If I were producing this show, I know that's where I'd plant it!"

"And," I said, "do you know how to find this field?"

Storm nodded. "I'm pretty sure. It'd be great if they gave us the same puzzle that the genius math teacher cracked. I memorized all his moves—the way you'd memorize the moves of a classic chess game."

"Really?" said Tommy. "People do that?"

"Only if they don't have a rigorous grooming regimen," said Storm.

"Yeah." Tommy swept back his hair so it was just right. "Looking this good can really burn into your free time."

I was feeling pretty pumped. If the producers did what Storm suspected they would, we might already have a head start for the next round of the competition.

The round we needed to win!

Beck, on the other hand, wasn't so psyched.

CHAPTER 26

"This stinks!" Beck exploded.

"What?" I said. "I changed my socks on the airplane."

"This whole thing stinks. Another fake treasure hunt?"

"It's a game, Beck!" I shouted. "We've been over this and over this. It. Is. A. Game!"

"No, Bick. It. Is. A. Waste. Of. Time!!!"

And we were off. We flew into Twin Tirade number 2,133. By the way, Twin Tirades are a lot worse in confined spaces like the back seats of an SUV. Those things are like echo chambers. I noticed the driver cranking up the volume on whatever he was listening to in an attempt to drown us out.

"A game is never a waste of time if we win!" I shrieked.

"But we usually play against each other! So, *we* can't win."

"*We* can this time! We might find out more info about our great-grandfather!"

"And, we might not!"

"Well, we can definitely show the world that we're better than the Collier kids!"

"Oh, great. We're better at finding phony treasure. Big whoop."

"Nobody says *big whoop* anymore, Rebecca."

"Well, they should."

"Yeah, it does have a certain ring to it."

"Especially inside this SUV."

"That's the echo," I told her.

Beck nodded. "So are we going to beat these Collier kids?"

"Definitely. We might even clear Great-Grandpa Joe's name for Dad."

"We better."

“I know.”

“Good.”

“Cool.”

“Sorry I got so upset, Bick.”

I shrugged. “No big whoop.”

Our SUV parked near an open plaza on the edge of the harbor village of Schaprode.

The Baltic Sea was splashing against the dock pilings and looking pretty spectacular. The island of Rügen was, according to Storm, a very popular tourist destination. It had sandy beaches, chalk cliffs, and “rejuvenating spas,” none of which we were interested in.

We were all about winning the game.

We formed a semicircle with the Collier kids in front of Dr. Hieronymus Whittley, who had a very picturesque church perched over his left shoulder. It probably made for good TV.

The village of Schaprode was a popular port for ferryboats to the island of Hiddensee (which sounded like it was named after the very popular game known as hide-and-seek). Storm said that the smaller island was car-free and another very popular tourist attraction. Except for the tourists who liked to drive cars.

The professor was giving us and the audience at home the same historical information about the Viking king's buried treasure that Storm had already given us, as well as the whole bit about Bluetooth technology being named after the guy because he was a great communicator and had a gnarly dead tooth that looked all dark and blue.

And, yes, I yawned a little. Maybe I should've dunked my head in some of that refreshing Baltic Sea water or headed off to a rejuvenating spa.

"I have in my possession," said the professor, "two copies of a puzzle written over a thousand years ago. It's a mathematical map left for King Harald Bluetooth's heirs so they might, one day, recover the silver coins, pearls, and other precious artifacts buried somewhere near here!"

I was trying hard not to smile. I didn't want to give away the fact that Storm was now our team's most valuable asset. I knew the professor was about to give us the same puzzle that the German math teacher had cracked. And Storm had memorized the guy's code-cracking moves. She'd be able to tell us where to search for this second treasure in a flash.

The professor dug two envelopes out of his tweed sport coat.

"We have translated the code into English since I don't believe any of you children read or speak Old Norse."

"Working on it!" Storm and Kioni said simultaneously.

"You will need proper math skills to crack this code," the professor said with a twinkle in his eye. "You may also need this."

He gestured to Bailey, our show runner. She gave each team a very touristy map of the area.

"Awesome," said Storm, checking out the map. "There's a horse stable run by a guy named Steffen Waak. We can go horseback riding."

"Um, maybe we can do that *after* we find the treasure?" I suggested.

"Fine," said Storm. "Whatever."

"Each team will also have a four-seater off-road vehicle for their use in this treasure quest," said Bailey. "The multi-terrain Polaris RZR Pro XP 4. It's the rugged off-road ride made famous in Pleyon's top-selling *Mud-Slingin' X-Treme Off-Roadin'* video game."

Beck and I gave each other a look. Now this fake treasure hunt had product placement shout-outs for bestselling Pleyon games, the show's sponsor? Could it get any cheesier?

"Who would like to solve the puzzle for each team?" asked the professor.

Storm shot up her hand. So did brainy Kioni.

Tommy was giving Kioni his flirty eyebrow wiggle-waggle. "Good luck," he said, because, basically, he couldn't help himself.

Beck slugged him in the arm to remind him which team he was on.

"Right," said Tommy, rubbing the sore spot. "My bad."

Kioni tore open the Collier team's envelope.

Storm ripped open ours.

Both brainiacs removed the coded message from its envelope. Storm nodded. And nodded. She also twiddled her fingers in the air as if she were working an invisible calculator.

Kioni stared blankly at the jumble of numbers on the sheet. She was not nodding or twiddling her digits. I could tell. She didn't have a clue as to what any of it meant.

"Are you certain that clue is in English?" snapped Kaiyo, the snarky one.

"Yes," said the professor. "And, as you can see, it's mostly numbers. Numbers are the same in both English and Old Norse."

"We'd like to ask an expert and phone a friend," said Carlos.

"Wrong game show," said Logan Bigelow, the director, from behind the camera.

Meanwhile, on our side of the semicircle, we were just waiting for Storm to confirm what we already knew.

"Got it," she said.

"Let's roll," said Tommy.

We took off, running for our four-seater ATV. Tommy hopped in behind the wheel. Storm called shotgun. Beck and I piled into the back. Our camera crew scrambled into their SUV to tail us.

"Where to?" Tommy asked Storm.

She tapped on the map.

"There! It's the field we're looking for."

"Got it."

"And," said Storm, pointing to a cartoon of a pony, "after we find the treasure, we'll celebrate our victory with a horse ride on the beach!!"

"Sounds like a plan!" said Tommy. He jammed his foot down on the accelerator. We blasted off.

"Whoo-hoo!" I shouted. "After two innings, this game is going to be all tied up."

Tommy glanced over his shoulder at me. "I thought this was a best two-out-of-three deal, not nine innings of baseball."

I was about to explain my mixed metaphor when Beck slapped me on the back. Repeatedly.

"What?" I asked, sounding annoyed because I was.

"Look!" said Beck. She pointed behind us. "Kioni Collier just wadded up her puzzle and tossed it to the ground. She's not even trying to crack the code. The four Collier kids are climbing into their ATV. They're going to follow us."

HEY, IF YOU CAN'T BEAT 'EM, CHEAT 'EM!
VROOM!
SCREECH!

Of course they are, I thought. *It's what people named Collier always do best. They let us Kidds find the treasure and then, somehow, steal it out from under us!*

And in this second round of the competition, the rules had changed. We were both working off the same clue.

CHAPTER 27

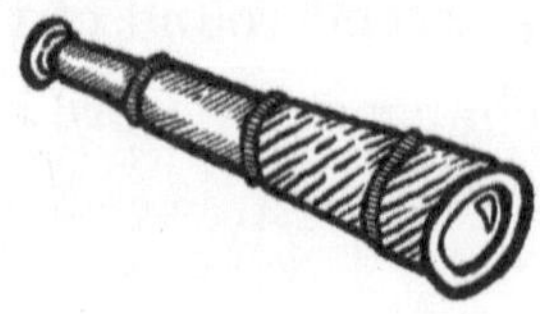

"This isn't fair!" I screamed as our ATV bounded up the cobblestone streets along the shoreline. "Both teams had the same clue this time. There aren't two separate paths to this treasure!"

"Your girlfriend Kioni is smart, Tommy," shouted Beck. "She knows they don't have to crack the code. All they have to do is follow us!"

"She's not that smart," said Storm. "Otherwise, she'd really be Tommy's girlfriend."

Tommy blushed a little. "Thanks, sis."

"So what do we do?" I asked. "We can't just

lead them to the field and wrestle them for the prize."

"Chya. That Kirk could totally take me. Even his fingernails have muscles."

"Well, we've got to do something!" shouted Beck, twisting back around in her seat. "They're gaining on us."

"Storm?" said Tommy, sounding like he did when he was up in the wheelhouse of our ship, ready to assume full command. "Plot out a course to that horse stable you found."

"On it."

"Then show Bick and Beck where they need to ride to find the treasure."

Storm flattened the map in her lap and used a marker to ink in a dotted route from the horse stables to the open field.

"Why are we going horseback riding?" I shouted. I wasn't angry, but ATVs don't have roofs or sides. You have to scream to be heard.

"Because," said Tommy, "we're going to divide and conquer. The Collier kids know Storm is the brains of our operation. So, she and I will go riding one way, maybe a nice scenic route along the beach. You two will head off in a different direction."

"But they'll just split up and follow us," said Beck.

Tommy shook his head as he twisted the steering wheel to take us down a bumpy dirt road. "No, they won't. Remember on that first plane ride? When Storm said she hoped we'd have a chance to go horseback riding…"

I thunked my head with my palm because I remembered what happened next. "Kaiyo said, 'We don't do horses. We prefer motorcycles and ATVs.'"

"Maybe they're allergic to horse dander," said Beck. "Or oats."

"Whatever the reason," said Tommy, "they're not gonna hop on a horse. They'll stick with their ATV."

"Which means," said Storm, "they can only follow after one set of riders. Tommy is correct. They will choose to pursue me. That will leave you guys free to go fetch the treasure!"

She handed me the map with the route to the treasure meadow. It made sense and would be easy to follow. Don't forget, we Kidds are big on nautical charts and treasure maps. We learned how to read those before we learned how to read *Hop on Pop*.

"We should pretend to have an argument," I said. "Let the Colliers see us splitting up."

"Yeah," said Beck. "Bick and I are good at yelling. We've done it thousands of times."

"Two thousand one hundred and thirty-three to be precise," I added.

"Those are just the Twin Tirades," said Beck.

"So?"

"So, we argue about other stuff all the time without launching into a full-blown tirade."

"Well," I said, "I don't count those."

"Well," said Beck, "maybe you should!"

"Or maybe *you* shouldn't..."

Fortunately, that's when Tommy cut the wheel hard to the right. We fishtailed a little and skidded into the parking lot of the Steffen Waak stables. The Colliers skidded in right behind us.

Storm hopped out first.

"The treasure isn't here!" she shouted at the Colliers.

"But we know where it is!" cried Tommy.

"No, you don't!" I hollered.

"Bick and I do!" screamed Beck.

"No, you don't!" said Tommy.

"Yes, we do!" said Beck.

"Fine," said Storm. "You two go your way, Tommy and I will go mine."

I stomped my feet and pouted. "But we only have one ATV!"

"No problem," said Tommy. "This is a stable. We'll rent horses and split up! You guys can keep the ATV."

"We want horses, too!" shouted Beck.

I gave her some side eye. I would've been fine sticking with the motorized vehicle. Saddles make my butt sore.

But, I played along.

The four of us headed into the offices to fill out liability forms, pick out our riding helmets, and pay for our rides. (Fortunately, Tommy has a Kidd Family Treasure Hunters LLC company credit card.)

It took like twenty minutes to get everything organized.

But the Colliers waited for us. They kept their ATV engine idling and their eyes glued on our every move. They'd be ready to take off the instant we did.

Finally, we saddled up and mounted our steeds.

"Do you need a map?" asked the nice German guy in charge of the horses.

"No, thank you," said Tommy. "We already have one."

"So do we," I said.

"Ours is better!" shouted Tommy, keeping up the fake argument.

"No, it's not!" I shouted back.

"May the best Kidds win!" said Storm. "Hiya!" She gave her steed a gentle kick. She and Tommy took off, galloping south.

"Hee-yah!" I cried, tugging my reins to the right. Beck matched my moves. In no time, we were heading north.

The Colliers made their choice.

Their ATV tires spat back a plume of dirt and gravel as they sped off to chase after Tommy and Storm. Both camera teams followed behind them.

I guess nobody in the game or on the production crew thought Beck and I knew what we were doing.

Fine.

I hoped they all enjoyed their time on the beach and took in the salty air of the Baltic Sea.

Meanwhile, Beck and I were off to enjoy the scenic view of an open field where the second treasure was just waiting for us to find it!

CHAPTER 28

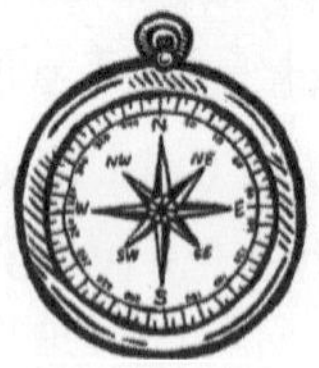

The horses moved swiftly, cantering along the route Storm had laid out on the map.

About twenty minutes after splitting off from Tommy and Storm, and with no Colliers or camera crews following us, Beck and I came to the open field. Weeds and flowers grew in furrows of rutted earth where heavy machinery like backhoes and bulldozers had scraped the dirt around during the big-time treasure extraction.

"Whoa," said Beck, pulling back on the reins of her horse.

"Whoa, Nelly," I said, because I'd decided to

give my horse a name. Plus, I'd always wanted to say "Whoa, Nelly" to an actual horse. My horse whickered and whinnied as he came to a halt. I don't think Nelly was his name.

"Looks like we came to the right place," I said.

"It's a field, Bick," said Beck. "A wide-open field. Do you see an X marking the spot where the treasure is buried?"

"No. But maybe if we walk around, we'll find some kind of clue."

"Or," said Beck, "maybe I should trade you in for a new brother."

My horse did one of those wet, lip-flapping snort things horses sometimes do. He nudged his head to the right.

"Whoa, Nelly," I said again.

But he wasn't listening. He just nickered and nudged harder. He basically pulled me off the trail so I could see something hidden behind a clump of trees.

"Good boy!" I said when I finally saw what my horse had already seen. I gave him a gentle pat on the side of his neck.

"Bick?" said Beck. "What are you doing down there in the weeds?"

"My horse saw something."

"Seriously?"

I nodded and pointed to what looked like a bike rack. There were eight metal detectors leaning up against it. Eight shiny shovels, too. The gold kind they use when they're breaking ground for a new building.

"It's the same kind of gear the first kid used to find the Viking king's loot when he came here with his math teacher!" I said.

Beck and her horse pranced over to see what I was seeing.

"I think the sun reflecting off those shovels must've caught Nelly's eye!" I said.

"Who's Nelly?" asked Beck.

I patted Nelly's neck again. "My horse."

"He's a stallion, Bick, not a mare."

"He's also the best horse in the world. Oh, yes he is. Oh, yes he is." I wished I had an apple or a sugar cube to give him. I pulled my feet out of the stirrups and swung off the saddle. "Come on, Beck. We have a meadow to metal detect!"

We tied our horses to a tree and grabbed metal detectors and shovels. My guess? The TV people had left the treasure-hunting gear where we'd find it so both teams would look ridiculous as we all combed the open field. It'd make for funny TV, especially if we started elbowing the Colliers and they started trying to trip us up.

Instead, it was just Beck and me, two metal detectors, a pair of gold-plated shovels, and a very large, wide-open field. It was going to take some time for us to comb the area and find whatever it was we were supposed to find. My guess? Something made of metal. Something, hopefully, besides a crushed soda pop can, bent spoon, or wadded-up ball of aluminum foil.

We strapped on the headphones attached to our ground-sweeping wands and went to work. I just hoped Tommy and Storm were leading the Colliers on a very long beach ride. Maybe they'd circle the entire island. Twice. Because this was going to be slooooow work.

Maybe twenty minutes later, Beck whipped off her headset and started yelling, "I found something!"

I ran to where she stood. She'd already scraped away a layer of mud to reveal a shining brass handle on what appeared to be a hinged, plywood trapdoor.

"Seriously?" I said. "Who puts a trapdoor in the middle of an open pasture?"

Suddenly, I heard the soft whirr of rotors overhead.

It was a camera drone.

Duh. This was all for the TV show.

"I guess this is the next move on the game board," I muttered.

Beck shook her head. "I can't wait to get back to real treasure hunting. Storm was right. This is like an escape room game."

"But we're doing it—"

"—for Dad's Grandpa Joe. I know, I know..."

We grabbed the handle and heaved it open.

We were staring down into a pitch-black pit.

"We need to jump!" said Beck.

"What? We can't see a thing. There might be snakes down there!"

"You really need to stop watching those Indiana Jones movies, Bick."

"What if there's nothing down there but jagged rocks? We could break every single bone in our bodies!"

Beck slipped a small flashlight out of a pocket in her shorts.

"That's why we carry these, remember?"

"Oh, right."

I pulled out my high-intensity flashlight, too. We shone both beams down into the hole. There was a huge, six-foot-thick, inflated airbag about ten yards below us. It would cushion our landing.

"That's what stunt artists use in Hollywood when they fake a fall," said Beck.

"And since this is a fake treasure hunt," I said, "they knew we'd need it to fake a leap into the pit."

"On three," said Beck.

We both counted down.

"One…two…three…"

We both leapt.

Then we both landed on our butts and bounced around as if the big air mattress were a trampoline.

When we settled, we swung our flashlights from side to side, searching for our "treasure."

"See anything?" said Beck.

"No, you?"

"Maybe. Hang on. Ha!"

"What?"

"Tommy would love this. It's Thor's hammer!"

CHAPTER 29

The instant Beck pulled the movie prop out of the muck, a thirty-three-foot step ladder rose up from the ground beside it.

The thing had some kind of cool hydraulics. Or maybe it was from a fire company's ladder truck.

"Congratulations!" boomed a voice at the top of our pit.

It was Bailey. Our show runner.

"Climb up and pretend we're not here," she said, gesturing to Logan and the camera crew that must've been hiding in the forest ringing the muddy field, waiting for somebody to find the trapdoor, jump into the hole in the ground, and claim this round's prize.

I nodded. I knew how to take direction.

"Come on, Beck," I said. "This is no Thordinary ladder!"

She groaned at my bad pun and we started climbing. She used one hand to haul herself up the rungs. The other was gripping Thor's hammer.

"Hey, how come you never laugh at my low-key jokes?" I quipped.

"Sorry, bro," she quipped back. "It's kind of a Thor subject."

Yeah. She could make up corny TV dialogue, too. Guess it's another twin thing.

Finally, we reached the top of the ladder. When we stepped off it and into the field, we were both beaming for the camera and the audience who, one day, would be watching us win the second round of the *World's Greatest Treasure-Hunting Kids!* competition.

A single word was chiseled into the silver head of the hammer:

GRATULERER

THIS WAS NO THORDINARY FEAT!
NOW EVERY DAY is THORSDAY!
GRATULERER

"I wonder what it means?" I said.

Beck shrugged. She had no idea, either.

"'Congratulations!'" said Professor Whittley, stepping out from behind the camera crew.

"Thank you," Beck and I said together.

"No," said the professor. "I'm not saying *congratulations*. I'm translating what *gratulerer* means in Norwegian."

"Oh," I said. "But, uh, we won this round, right?"

"Yes," boomed the professor. "Congratulations!"

This time, he wasn't just translating.

CHAPTER 30

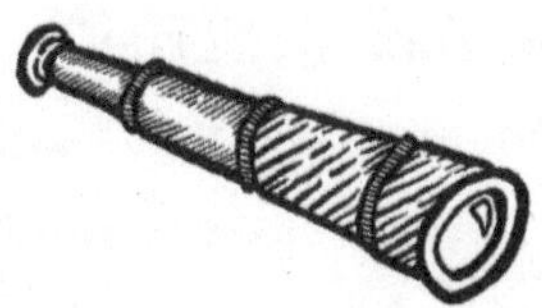

Tommy and Storm joined us about thirty minutes later. The Collier kids arrived with them.

We Kidds had a little victory celebration in the open field. The TV people brought out the party props. We had snacks and soda and music. And cake. The cake was awesome. Beck and I took turns holding the Thor hammer. It was pretty heavy. So we handed it off to Tommy. He one-arm curled it a few times to pump up his biceps.

"Way to go, Bick and Beck," he said between hoists and grunts.

"Hey, it wasn't all us," I said.

"Storm's the one who figured it out," said Beck.

"And," said Storm, "you, Tommy, were the one

who came up with the extremely clever divide-and-conquer battle tactic that took the Colliers out of the game!"

"True," said Tommy. "True."

"You misled me, Tommy," said the beautiful Kioni. "In fact, I dare say you double-crossed me."

Tommy dropped his head. He looked slightly heartbroken. But, then he grinned.

"Chya. Guess I did. Usually it's the other way around. Pretty girls always double-cross me."

"So how does it feel to be the double-crosser

matched his moves. The real treasure of the Viking king was found years ago. At best, we were merely players in a historical reenactment. *Nisi utile est quod facimus, stulta est gloria*," she reminded us. "Unless what we do is useful, glory is foolish."

"Well," said Beck, "if, in the next round, we can somehow redeem our great-grandfather's name for whatever terrible thing he did, that would be useful, right?"

Storm nodded. "Indeed. And so, we play on."

"With Pleyon!" said Tommy.

"All competitors?" said Bailey. "We have a bus to take us back to the airfield. Our next stop will be another Baltic Sea resort—Ustka, Poland."

"What's there?" asked Beck.

"Your next challenge, Rebecca. And, your parents."

CHAPTER 31

To get to Ustka we had to take an overnight flight to Gdańsk.

For some reason, people in Poland are pretty skimpy with their vowels. They like to slam a lot of consonants up against each other and dare you to figure out how to pronounce cities like Ustka and Gdańsk.

"Ustka is too tiny to have its own airport," said Kioni as we flew on the private jet.

"True," said Storm. "As of 2001, there were only seventeen thousand one hundred inhabitants."

Not to be outdone, Kioni said, "Plus one mermaid."

Storm gave Kioni a smirky look. "I assume you are referring to Ustecka Syrenka, the bronze statue unveiled in 2010, which sits on a marble pedestal on the harbor pier?"

Kioni bristled a little. The rest of us were set to watch another brainy volley, pinging and ponging across the jet's center aisle.

"You are correct," Kioni admitted. Then added, "Syrenka, of course, is Polish for mermaid."

"True," said Storm. She had the look on her face she always gets when she's just about to slam somebody with her trivia game. "But there is more than one syrenka, or mermaid, in Ustka. She is also on the town's coat of arms and its flags. She wears a crown and holds a salmon in her hand."

"Ew," said Tommy.

"Gross," added Kirk.

"I hope this mermaid has hand sanitizer," snarked Kaiyo.

"Actually," said Storm, "the salmon is part of a larger legend of how the mermaid of pure heart named Bryzga Rosowa took pity on a blind widow."

"The mermaid's heart was named Bryzga?" cracked Carlos.

"No," said Storm. Dark clouds of anger billowed up in her eyes.

It was time to change the subject. Fast.

"So," I said, standing up and pulling the Thor trophy out of my carry-on bag. "You see this word? That's Norwegian. For congratulations."

"We know," said Kaiyo. "You've told us a billion times."

"You want to see our crown again?" said Carlos.

"Nah," said Beck. "It doesn't have any cool Norwegian words stamped on it."

"Because," said Kioni, getting huffy, "we found *our* treasure in England!"

"Enjoy it," I said. "Because it's the last treasure you're going to find in this competition!"

The longer we were in the air, the more the trash talk flew back and forth across the aisle.

"We're gonna crush you in this final round!" cried Kaiyo. Actually, she kind of shrieked it. The kid has a very high-pitched, very loud voice.

"Ha!" I said. "Ha, ha, ha." Yeah, for a word guy, I sometimes run out of them.

"Two things, Bick," Kaiyo screeched back at me. "One—where have you been all my life? Two—can you please go back there? Pronto?"

Storm rolled her eyes at that one.

"Oh, yeah," said Kaiyo. "Keep rolling your eyes, Storm. Maybe you'll find a brain back there." Next, she turned to Beck. "When I say you're a loser, Beck, I'm not insulting you. I'm describing you."

"Whoa," said Tommy, looking up from his phone. "Dial it down a notch."

"Yeah, Kaiyo," added Kirk.

Kaiyo gave both big brothers a very snarky look. "Remember when I asked you two for your opinion?" she said. "Yeah. Me neither."

Tommy shook his head and whispered across the aisle to Kirk. "Dude, your little sister is off the chain."

Kirk shrugged. "Hey, every reality TV show needs a villain. Kaiyo is ours."

"What about me?" demanded Carlos. "I'm mean and nasty, too."

"Nah," said Kaiyo. "You, Carlos, are the reason they have to put instructions on bottles of shampoo."

Fortunately, the jet (eventually) landed in Gdańsk.

The bus ride from the airport to our hotel was, mercifully, quiet. I guess little Kaiyo was all out of snark juice.

We stepped off the bus, ready to learn what our next and final challenge might be. Kirk turned to Tommy.

"It all comes down this," he said.

"Chya," said Tommy. "Whatever *this* is. May the best team win."

"How sweet, Thomas," said Kioni with a snide, sideways smile. "You're rooting for us!"

CHAPTER 32

The Hotel Rejs, where we'd be staying, was located on a quiet street in the historic city center of Ustka.

(I wondered if all the streets were quiet in Ustka—since vowels are where words can get loud.)

The hotel was maybe two blocks from the Stupia river, which empties into the Baltic Sea. The sea was only an eight-minute walk away. Same thing with that mermaid statue on its shoreline. You know—the fish lady with the slimy salmon in her hand.

"Your parents are waiting for you inside the

conference room," said Bailey. She and the rest of the *World's Greatest Treasure-Hunting Kids!* TV production crew had flown earlier on commercial airlines to Gdańsk and were already checked into their rooms.

I checked out the hotel's fancy exterior. It looked like a ginormous Bavarian manor. The kind you see in cuckoo clocks.

"Why are Mom and Dad going to be involved in this final round of the competition?" Storm asked Bailey as we clacked across the hotel's marble lobby. "Isn't the objective to declare one group of *children* the World's Greatest Treasure-Hunting Kids?"

"Not sure," said Bailey. "But, I suspect it has something to do with making sure the kids in our viewing audience always seek out adult supervision before undertaking dangerous activities such as the ones you children are demonstrating in the show."

I nodded. That made sense. Of course, we Kidd kids had already undertaken some pretty incredibly dangerous activities on our own—but mostly during the long stretch of time when none of our adults were available for supervision duties because they'd been kidnapped or washed overboard in a tropical storm. Also, we're like the Wild Things in that picture book. We're always up for a wild rumpus.

Mom and Dad were waiting for us in the big conference room. It was great to see them!

We raced together for a huge hug!

"Here they are!" said Mom. "My favorite treasure-hunting kids in the whole wide world!"

"Well done on that German island, team!" added Dad.

Then we all brought it in for another big family group hug.

While we were hugging it out, I couldn't help noticing that Nathan Collier and his kids were, well, a little less emotional about their family reunion.

"Here you go, Kirk," I heard Collier say as he handed his incredible hulk of a son a large envelope—one of those ones with the string tie clasps. "You'll find a little something extra in your allowance envelope this week."

BICK?
HAVE YOU BEEN
USING THAT
DEODORANT I
BOUGHT FOR YOU?
WELCOME TO
MY STINKY
NIGHTMARE,
MOM.

"Thank you, Mr. Collier," said Kirk eagerly.

Wow. What a weird family. I don't think I'd ever call my dad Mr. Kidd. For one thing, he has a PhD. So, I'd have to call him Dr. Kidd. For another, he likes being called Dad more than anything else.

As we broke out of our group snuggle, I kept one eye on Collier as he handed the next allowance envelope to Kioni. "Well played in round two, young lady," I heard him say. "You earned an allowance bump, too!"

"Thank you," said Kioni, taking her envelope. "I hoped you might be pleased with the outcome."

Okay. Things were getting even weirder. The Colliers *lost* the second round. Why was Nathan Collier so happy about Kioni not being able to figure out the mathematical code as quickly as Storm had?

"Something's fishy," I whispered to Beck. "And it's not that mermaid statue."

"I know," she whispered back. "I get a whiff of it every time we do a family hug. Deodorant, Bick. De-o-dor-ant!"

"I mean something's not right with the Collier kids."

"Well, duh. They're all pretty obnoxious."

I head nodded toward Kaiyo. She had opened her envelope and wasn't happy with whatever was in it.

"Nathan?" she said. "I need to make a phone call. To Mommy."

"It can wait," Collier seethed through his teeth.

"Uh, no, it can't."

"What's all that fuss at the other end of the table?" said Dad. Nathan Collier's interaction with the Collier kids had caught his attention. Mom's too.

"Did Kaiyo just call her father Nathan?" asked Storm.

"Chya," said Tommy. "A lot of cool kids do that. Their parents are like their friends instead of authority figures."

Now Mom and Dad were staring at Tommy.

"Did I say a lot of cool kids did it?" he quickly back pedaled. "I meant a lot of *fool* kids. I know *I'd* never call you guys Susan and Tom. For one thing, I'd think I was talking to myself because Tom is short for Tommy."

Yes, Tommy was blubbering. Fortunately for him that's when the contest's corporate sponsor, the president and CEO of Pleyon, Mertin Schmerkel, marched into the room.

CHAPTER 33

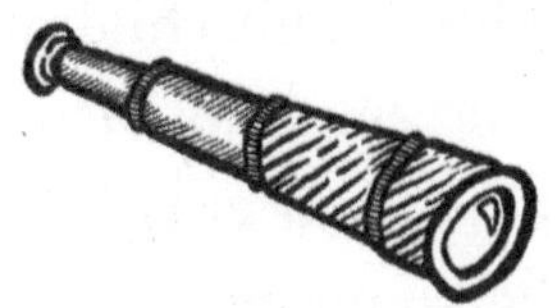

"Good afternoon to you all, industrious and diligent treasure-hunting children," said Mr. Schmerkel.

He clicked his bootheels together and dipped into a quick bow. Kaiyo quit fussing with her "allowance envelope." She wasn't heading out to the lobby to call Mommy anymore, either. Mr. Schmerkel was a very imposing, very commanding figure.

"*Mein Kinder*, I have been most impressed by your *Zielstrebigkeit*, *militarische Disziplin*, and your *Mut*!"

"Did someone bring a dog?" wondered Tommy.

Mom and Dad chuckled a little. "Those are German words," said Dad.

"Storm?" said Mom. "Translation, please."

"First he called us his children. Then he said he admired our single-minded determination, military discipline, and grit. Or courage. Maybe pluck. Could be spunkiness. The German word *Mut* has all sorts of meanings."

"But none of them are dogs?" asked Tommy.

"Correct," said Storm.

"Good."

"Why is a Polish man speaking German?" I asked.

"I was going to ask the same thing," said Beck.

"But I asked it first. Probably because I'm older than you."

"By like half a minute."

"Still..."

Storm stepped in to stop another Twin Tirade before it got started. "Maybe he likes using words with more than one meaning."

While Storm was translating and we Kidds

were chatting among ourselves, Mr. Schmerkel was peering at us very intently. That peering was made even more intense by the fact that he was sporting a monocle—which is like half of a pair of eyeglasses but without any frames or earpieces. Just one lens pinched between his cheek and the top of his eye socket.

Did I mention the fact that he had a huge, walrus mustache? It looked like he was sniffing a rope. And his hair? I think he asked his barber for the "scrub brush special."

"Children," the Polish billionaire continued, "we at Pleyon have been very impressed by your competitive spirit. You are to be rewarded this day with a feast."

He clapped his two meaty hands together. Twice.

"Play on!" said Kirk.

"With Pleyon!" added Tommy.

"You two muscular children are my favorites!" said Schmerkel with a rumbling, manly chuckle. "And not simply because you know my advertising slogan. You are my modern Potsdam Giants."

"He's not swearing," Mom whispered.

"Potsdam is the capital and largest city in the German state of Brandenburg," added Storm.

And then Kioni butted in because of course she did. "Johann Sebastian Bach wrote the Brandenburg concertos."

Schmerkel turned to the conference room's open door. "*Żywność!*" he bellowed. "*Ale już!*"

"Now he's speaking Polish," said Storm.

"He said, 'Food! Now!'" added Kioni.

"I was about to tell them that," said Storm.

“*Śpisz, przegrywasz,*” said Kioni. “That’s Polish for ‘You snooze, you lose.’”

Storm scrunched up her face like she wanted to stick out her tongue.

At Schmerkel’s command, several uniformed servers marched into the meeting room carrying steaming platters of food. None of it smelled very good. Most of it smelled like vinegar. And dirt. Or dirt mixed with vinegar.

“Let us eat, children!” Schmerkel declared. “Boiled meatballs with boiled potatoes! Pickled beet soup! Bratwurst and onion cooked in vinegar and served with Bavarian pretzels!”

Well, at least the pretzels sounded edible.

We sat down on one side of the long table, the Colliers on the other. Mr. Schmerkel sat at the head of the table, and between slurps of bright red soup and dips of pretzel into the vinegar sauce, he told us the big news. “In this final round of the contest, the training wheels will be coming off. No more silly make-believe treasure hunts for cheap plastic crowns and imitation Thor hammers. This, as you say in America, is the real deal. The genuine article. The no-joke McCoy."

"Nobody in America says that," Beck whispered out of the side of her mouth.

Schmerkel didn't hear her. Probably because he was making a lot of noise chewing mushy meatballs.

"This final round is for all the marbles," he said, using his napkin to blot at the sour cream stuck in his whiskers. "A true treasure quest. This is why your parents have been invited to participate in the final challenge. One of your two families—the Colliers or the Kidds—will not only be crowned the World's Greatest Treasure-Hunting Kids. You will soon discover one of the world's most amazing, most incredible, most still-missing treasures."

He plucked out his monocle to make his pronouncement even more dramatic.

"The fabled Amber Room! The Eighth Wonder of the World!"

CHAPTER 34

I was about to remind Mr. Schmerkel that Mom and Dad weren't kids so maybe he needed to come up with a new title for his TV show.

But I noticed Mom and Dad exchanging a glance. It was one of those where I know they know more than what they've let us know they know. They had some sort of shared secret and seemed eager to hear whatever Mr. Schmerkel had to say about the Amber Room.

The big man put down his silverware, pushed back from the table, and stood up. With hands clasped behind his back, he paced back and forth like a general in the command tent on the night before a big battle.

"As I am sure many of you know, the jewel-studded Amber Room was built in eighteenth-century Prussia."

Mom, Dad, Nathan Collier, Storm, and Kioni were all nodding. They were the treasure history buffs in the room. I just knew that the Amber Room had been on Mom and Dad's "Top Ten List of Missing Treasures" in The Room on board our ship for as long as I could remember. It was right up there with the tomb of Genghis Khan, the Honjo Masamune sword, and Dad's purple-and-green argyle socks. (Those have been missing since an unfortunate event at a laundromat in Shanghai.)

"In 1716," Schmerkel continued, "the Prussian king, Friedrich Wilhelm the First, presented the Russian emperor with a room designed by the most talented Prussian architects and sculptors. A room decorated with amber and gold and sparkling with precious jewels. This amazing gift was packed into eighteen large boxes, shipped east, and rebuilt inside the Catherine Palace near St. Petersburg."

"The one in Russia," I said.

MIX RED WITH YELLOW TO MAKE AMBER.
AMBER IS HALFWAY BETWEEN YELLOW AND ORANGE ON THE COLOR WHEEL. BICK'S NOSE IS HALFWAY BETWEEN GREEN AND BOOGER.

"Not Florida," added Beck. We slapped each other high five. (We did the same routine anytime anybody mentioned St. Petersburg.)

"Amber's that golden gemstone from *Jurassic Park*," said Tommy. "The see-through gunk with the mosquito fossils stuck inside it."

"Actually," said Storm, "amber is fossilized tree resin. And, technically, it's not a gemstone. But amber crystals have been carved into jewelry for thousands of years."

"Waves of grain are also sometimes called amber," said Kioni.

Mr. Schmerkel kept plowing ahead with his historical monologue.

"Unfortunately, the Amber Room was seized by the Nazis during World War II. The room's glorious panels were disassembled, packed into crates, and shipped to the city of Königsberg."

When Schmerkel said *Königsberg*, I swear I heard DUN-DUN-DUN music.

I flashbacked to that thick Königsberg folder Mom and Dad kept in The Room.

"Königsberg is where the Amber Room was

last seen in 1945," said Schmerkel. He turned to face Dad. "I believe your grandfather was in Königsberg near the end of World War II?"

Dad nodded. "That is correct."

Schmerkel shook his head. "It's a shame he could not save the Amber Room. But, fortunately, I have recently come into possession of some new information. A new clue. A chance for one of your two families to go down in the history books as the treasure hunters who finally found the long-lost Amber Room and corrected Joseph Kidd's foolish blunder!"

CHAPTER 35

Dad's shoulders sagged.

His head drooped. The family burden, whatever it was, seemed to weigh him down more than the Prussian meatballs dive-bombing into our bellies.

"Whoa," I said. "Can we lay off the foolish blunder stuff?"

"Yeah," echoed Beck.

Neither one of us had ever met our great-grandfather, but his last name was Kidd. That means he was family. You don't trash-talk our family. (Unless you're in the family, then it's considered good-natured ribbing or an important part of a healthy Twin Tirade.)

You definitely don't do it when they're not around to defend themselves.

"Our great-grandfather Joseph Kidd," said Storm, in that calm and steady voice she uses when you know she'd rather be screaming, "was one of the famous Monuments Men of World War II."

"Was he made out of stone or bronze?" sniped Kaiyo.

"Neither," replied Storm. "He was a member of a special force of art historians who, near the end of World War II, risked their lives trying to prevent the Nazis from destroying thousands of years of art and culture."

"And," added Tommy, striking a double-guns bodybuilder pose, "if anybody in this room wants to trash-talk my great-grandfather, bring it on. I *am* made out of stone."

"So am I," said Kirk. "I also have buns of steel."

"Okay. Let me, uh, rephrase my warning. If anybody in this room who isn't Kirk wants to trash-talk my great-grandfather..."

Dad stood up and silenced Tommy with a gently raised hand.

"We are all very proud of Joseph Kidd," said Dad. "My grandfather was very inspirational. In fact, he was the reason I decided to become a treasure hunter."

"Because you knew it would be easy to be way better at it than he was?" cracked Carlos.

"I warned you, little dude!" said Tommy, leaping to his feet.

"Thomas?" said Mom.

Tommy sat back down.

Mertin Schmerkel pounded a clenched fist into his open palm. "Enough of this bickering!" he barked, and focused his monocled gaze on Dad. "I know you would like to clear your grandfather's good name by being the one to find the Amber Room's pilfered and plundered precious panels."

He spat out every one of those popping *p* sounds. (The way we Kidds like to spit out the *k* sound whenever we say *Collier.*)

He knuckled his fists into the table and leaned

forward. "Do you, Professor Thomas Kidd, have any new information on the lost treasure's whereabouts?"

Dad shrugged. "Sorry."

"We have no new intelligence," added Mom.

"Sure," said Dad, "the Amber Room has been on our list of lost treasures for years. But it's never really been a top priority."

Schmerkel clucked his tongue and shook his head. "What a pity. I would have assumed that restoring the honor of your family's name would have become your primary goal in life."

Dad shrugged again. "Nope. Hate to disappoint you. But it wasn't and isn't."

"Ha!" laughed Nathan Collier. "Ha, ha, ha!"

His kids Carlos and Kaiyo blew lip farts of disbelief. Kioni was shaking her head disappointedly. Kirk tried to shake his head, too, but his neck muscles were too thick to allow very much back-and-forth action.

I didn't totally believe Dad, either.

I kept remembering that scene Beck and I witnessed in The Room.

Mom and Dad poring over that file labeled "Königsberg Castle."

Mom telling Dad to *Cheer up. No treasure has to remain lost forever.*

So, yeah. Mertin Schmerkel was on to something. No matter what he said, finding the Amber Room would always be at the top of Dad's "To Do" list.

“Well,” said Schmerkel, easing into his hands-clasped-behind-his-back pacing mode, “fortunately for you, Herr Professor Thomas Kidd, I *do* have some new intelligence. It seems that a German ship called the *Karlsruhe*, sunk by Russian bombers in 1945, was recently found by Polish divers at the bottom of the Baltic Sea. We have reason to believe that the Amber Room is in the cargo hold of that shipwreck!”

CHAPTER 36

"For this final round of the competition," Schmerkel continued, "once your boats are in the Baltic, there will be no camera crews following either team. Nothing to slow you down or get in your way. We will 're-create' the action of the quest with a reenactment by the winning team—after they have won."

The Colliers were all nodding. They seemed fine with the new rules.

On our side of the table, we were, of course, more interested in the actual treasure hunt than the TV show.

"You may choose any seafaring vessel you

like," said Schmerkel, "and I will have it airlifted and dropped wherever you would like to start your quest. Unfortunately, the Polish divers did not give me the precise location of their underwater discovery."

Tommy raised his hand. "You're going to fly our boat, *The Lost Again*, up from where it's docked and drop it into the Baltic Sea?"

"Yes," said Mr. Schmerkel.

"This is just like in your Pleyon video game!" said Kirk. "*Extreme Battle Stations*! Where the cargo plane drops the spongy aircraft carrier into the ocean."

"And," said Tommy, "then the thing expands to full size once it hits the salt water. Sort of like those magic-grow giant crocodiles I used to play with in the bathtub!"

Schmerkel beamed. "Precisely."

"I believe we'll be taking Mr. Collier's submarine," said Kioni. "It is the most logical choice since the *Karlsruhe* is currently under the water."

"We have a brand-new, compact submarine on our ship," countered Storm. "A six-seater. I feel confident we will be using it to find the shipwreck before you and the rest of the Collier crew find a sunken boot or old tire."

"Save the boasting for after you find the Amber Room," sneered Collier. "Mr. Schmerkel failed to ask me if I had any new intelligence on the whereabouts of the *Karlsruhe*."

"And do you?" asked Dad skeptically.

"Oh, yes, Thomas," said Mr. Collier. "I know exactly what to do and where to go."

"Then," said Dad, "may the best treasure-hunting family win."

It took a couple of days for the logistics to be worked out.

Our ship, *The Lost Again*, was still docked in Port Said, that Egyptian city on the coast of the Mediterranean Sea, just north of the Suez Canal. The boat was so big, it took three whole hours for Schmerkel's air crew to load it into the cargo compartment of their jumbo-sized transport plane.

None of the Colliers would let on about where

their "vessel" was docked. When the competition started back up, they'd be boarding the Nathan Collier Treasure Extractors submarine that Tommy, Storm, Beck, and I had bumped into in the Caribbean Sea on one of our earlier adventures.

Logan and his camera crew grabbed a few shots of us studying maps and nautical charts and making faces while we sampled the sauer klopse that Mr. Schmerkel insisted that the hotel kitchen serve us for lunch. Every day.

"It is Prussian meatball soup!" he said. "It will make you strong for the coming battle."

After picking up that sort of "behind the scenes" footage, the camera crews took off.

"We'll see you when we come back for the reenactment," said Bailey.

On our final afternoon in Ustka, Mom and Dad had a top secret meeting with Mertin Schmerkel and his loadmasters about where, precisely, they would like our ship to be airdropped. I, once again, had a feeling that our parental units knew something about this shipwreck that we didn't. Something major.

They also needed Schmerkel's help because they needed the gear on board *The Lost Again.*

The next morning, we all climbed into a bus and headed east to the Lądowisko Nowęcin airstrip on the southern shore of the Baltic Sea.

The Colliers climbed into one helicopter.

We climbed into the other.

"Hey, Kidds?" shouted Carlos before he and his sibs took off. "Be sure to follow me on TikTok and Knick-Knock. I'm CarlosTheCool on both platforms. You can also subscribe to my YouTube channel and Instagram page. I really don't do Facebook. Don't need to. I have a bajillion followers. Hit me up if you ever have any fresh content you need me to boost. I'm sending you my deets."

I nodded. It seemed to be the polite thing to do even though Carlos was acting extremely weirdly. Two seconds later, my phone dinged. I had the deets. Even though I wanted them like I wanted beets.

Mertin Schmerkel stood stiffly between the two whirlybirds as their rotors started spinning.

The tips of his walrus mustache fluttered in the downdraft.

"May the best treasure-hunting family win!" he shouted.

"He means us!" shouted Kaiyo.

"In your dreams!" Beck shouted back.

We might've erupted into a two-family tirade, but both choppers lifted off.

The Colliers headed west by northwest. We flew east by northeast.

"We're heading in opposite directions," observed Storm through her helicopter helmet microphone. "Is it possible the Colliers know something that we don't?"

We all let that question hang in the air for maybe ten seconds.

Then, we burst into laughter.

"Yeah. Right. Like that'll ever happen."

Twenty minutes later, Dad came over our headsets. It's the only way to talk in a noisy helicopter.

"We're approaching the drop zone. Give the parachute one final check, gang."

That's right. *The Lost Again* wasn't the only thing dropping into the Baltic Sea. We'd be parachuting down right behind it.

And, if we all remembered what we'd learned in jump school a few years back, with any luck, none of us would get our feet wet. We'd all land on the deck of our ship!

CHAPTER 37

I touched down before anybody else.

It might've been because I had that Thor hammer tucked inside my backpack. It gave me a little extra weight and what Storm called "extra drag force" on my end of the chute.

I put the shimmering hammer in the trophy case we have in the galley of our new ship. I propped it next to the "You Tried" trophy Beck picked up at a karaoke contest in Korea.

Okay, fine. Beck says I have to tell you I sang so badly at the same contest that I didn't even take home a tiny loving cup like hers. They gave

me bronze earplugs. And a plaque that said, PLEASE DON'T TRY AGAIN.

We all stowed our gear in our cabins and then gathered up in the wheelhouse. Mom and Dad told Tommy to lay in a course for coordinates that "certain friends of ours shared with us."

I raised my hand.

"Yes, Bickford?" said Mom.

"Were these certain friends, by any chance, certain Polish divers?"

"Yes," said Mom. "And it seems that news of their discovery at the bottom of the Baltic Sea—which, by the way, we helped orchestrate—somehow reached Mertin Schmerkel. But, only the 'Baltic Sea' part of it."

"Even with all his money," added Dad, "Schmerkel couldn't buy anything more meaningful than that top-line information. Too bad the Baltic Sea is so huge."

Storm took that as her cue for another info dump. "It is approximately nine hundred and ninety miles long and an average of one hundred and twenty miles wide."

Mom smiled. "Making the square mileage the sea covers what, Stephanie?"

"The surface area of the Baltic Sea is about one hundred forty-nine thousand square miles—give or take a square mile or two."

"Correct."

Tommy whistled. "That's a whole lot of area to cover. The Colliers won't know where to start!"

"Um, do we?" I asked.

"Yes," said Dad. "We know exactly where to go.

As your mother indicated, we're the ones who told the deep-sea divers from Poland where to look for the shipwreck. Because we're the ones who want to rescue it for posterity, not profit. Turn her about, Tommy. We'll be laying in a zigzag course, just to make sure nobody is following us."

"Aye, aye, Cap'n!" said Tommy. He loves a good zigzag course.

As we cut across the choppy water, Mom and Dad kept homeschooling us with a quick history lesson about the 196-foot-long steamer known as the SS *Karlsruhe*, currently lying at the bottom of the Baltic.

"It took part in the massive German evacuation of East Prussia in April 1945, near the end of the Second World War," said Mom.

"The Nazis called it Operation Hannibal," added Dad. "They were losing the war and retreating as quickly as they could from the Soviet Union's advancing Red Army."

Mom picked up the wartime tale. "The *Karlsruhe* was the last German ship to leave Königsberg in East Prussia—what's now Kaliningrad in Russia."

"Does Prussia even exist anymore?" asked Tommy.

"No," said Dad. "Parts of it are in modern-day Poland, Lithuania, Russia, and Germany. Anyway, the *Karlsruhe* steamed west, but it was sunk by Soviet warplanes one day after it left port."

Mom showed us a picture of the doomed German ship.

"Many historians have long speculated that among the cargo loaded into the ship as it fled were several wooden crates containing the dismantled jigsaw puzzle pieces of priceless panels that made up the Amber Room."

"And the *Karlsruhe* was the last ship out of Königsberg?" said Tommy.

"Yes. If the Nazis wanted to sneak out a valuable treasure, the *Karlsruhe* was their last chance to do it."

CHAPTER 38

"To be honest, gang, this was always going to be our next treasure hunt," said Dad. "But, well, we saw how much you kids wanted to defend your reputations against the viral video onslaught of the Collier kids."

"Chya," said Tommy. "Totally. Those dudes and dudettes were making us look bad."

(And looking bad is something Tommy never wants to do. It's why he has so many different kinds of hair gel.)

"Well," said Mom, "as it turns out, we can now achieve two goals at once. You kids can show the world that you're much better treasure hunters than those four Collier children."

"Booyah!" Beck and I gave that a double arm pump.

"And," said Dad, "we can also, perhaps, redeem my grandfather's reputation."

"Was he responsible for the Amber Room winding up on that sunken Nazi cargo ship?" asked Storm.

"Partially, I suppose," said Dad. "As you know, my granddad, Joseph 'Jumpin' Joe' Kidd, was a professor of archaeology at Princeton University. He was also a trained paratrooper. He was as smart as Storm, as athletic as Tommy, and as feisty as Bick and Beck. He also spoke fluent Russian. Near the end of the war, when he joined the Monuments Men, he volunteered to work with the Russian army as they retook territory the Nazis had occupied."

I suddenly remembered the photograph. The one we'd found hidden in the secret compartment of that metal box Tommy retrieved from the Porty John in England. The American and Russian aviators from World War II shaking hands over a pile of bombs hashtagged "Hitler." That was our great-grandfather, Joseph Kidd, and his Russian Monuments Men counterpart.

Tommy showed the photo to Dad.

"That's him," said Dad. "And, most likely, Sergei."

"Who's Sergei?" I asked.

"Grandpa Joe's Russian counterpart. As a

battle raged on the streets of the city, Grandpa Joe and his new friend, the art historian Sergei, entered Königsberg Castle. Sergei told Grandpa Joe how, a few days earlier, he'd noticed fragments of a wall panel and a mirror framed in amber hanging inside the castle's Knights Hall. They found the castle's custodian and asked him about this evidence of the Amber Room. It was a very uneasy conversation. Bombs were exploding all over the city. The castle walls shook with each blast. The halls and chambers were filled with dust, rubble, and falling debris."

"Whoa," said Tommy. "Poor custodian. How was he ever going to clean up a mess like that? Were there vacuum cleaners in 1945?"

"Yes," said Storm.

Dad kept going. "The terrified custodian told Grandpa Joe and Sergei that the Nazi occupiers had stored the rest of the amber paneling in crates in the basement. The three of them were about to retrieve the treasure when another bomb or tank blast—some kind of explosion—scored a direct hit on the castle! A heavy stone column toppled sideways and pinned the custodian to the floor. It nearly crushed the old man's legs. Working together, and improvising a lever out of an antique knight's lance, Grandpa Joe and Sergei were able to free the injured man and drag him outside to safety.

"But they couldn't go back into the castle. It was engulfed in flames. Black smoke filled the skies above it. Bombs kept exploding. Machine guns kept firing. Grandpa Joe and Sergei vowed to return the next day—after the shelling and bombing died down. After the final battle for Königsberg was won by the Red Army."

"Did they?" I asked.

Dad nodded. "Yes. But whatever had been in the cellar was long gone. There weren't any crates. No jewel-encrusted amber panels or golden statues."

"Because," said Mom, "if we are correct, it had all been packed in the hold of a cargo ship. The SS *Karlsruhe*."

"In my opinion," said Dad, "Grandpa Joe made the right choice. He saved a man's life instead of saving the treasure. But, well, he never lived down the fact that the Nazis snuck one of the most important historical artifacts the world had ever known right out from under his nose."

We all nodded. The wheelhouse grew eerily quiet.

What would we have done? Saved a stranger's life or the Eighth Wonder of the World?

Suddenly, Dad interrupted the silence.

"Stop the engines, Tommy!" he barked.

Tommy did.

"Um, why are we stopping?" I asked.

"Because, Bick, the SS *Karlsruhe* and, hopefully, the long-lost Amber Room, are now directly below us. It's time we went down to salvage the treasure *and* our family's good name!"

CHAPTER 39

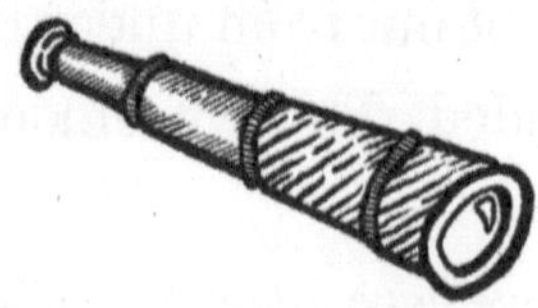

We quickly deployed our shiny new six-seater minisub.

It looked like a big glass bubble crossed with a ginormous snowblower powered by rockets. The sub was fully pressurized so there was no need to pack our scuba gear. We lowered it into the water off our stern. It bobbed up and down in the waves like a high-tech beach ball.

"Hopefully," said Dad, "we'll be able to poke around in the shipwreck with the sub's robotic grabber arms." He gestured toward two impressive-looking articulated claws jutting out from under the sub's nose.

"How deep will we be diving?" asked Tommy.

"Eighty-eight meters," said Mom. "Straight down."

Dad pressed a button on a small remote. Circular sections on both sides of the submarine's bubble pod slid up.

"All aboard," said Dad. And, yes, he did it like a train conductor. Sometimes, he also wears Dad jeans and tells Dad jokes like, *Where do pirates get their hooks? Second hand stores.*

"Let's go hunt some treasure!" I said.

The six of us climbed down a rope ladder and slid into the bobbing submarine. We strapped ourselves into our assigned seats. Mom would do the navigating. Tommy would drive the sub.

"The rest of us need to keep an eye out for unexploded munitions," said Dad.

"Um, excuse me?" Beck and I said at the same time.

"There are three hundred thousand tons of bombs, mines, and shells rotting away in the Baltic Sea," Storm reported with a bored eye roll, as if everybody in the world already knew that particular factoid. "Most of it is left over from World War II."

"So," said Tommy, "we might bump into a few of the unexploded bombs that the Russians tried to drop on our German cargo ship before they dropped the big one that sank it?"

"Correct," said Mom.

Great, I thought. *It's like we're playing a game of Battleship but with real hits and misses.*

"Keep your eyes peeled, everybody," coached Dad as Tommy took us down into the murky waters of the Baltic Sea. As our submarine dove and purred along, all we saw were fish. And seaweed. And fish snacking on seaweed.

Pretty soon, we reached the bottom and scooted along the seafloor, which was swirling with weedy stuff. It was a pretty dull and routine ride.

Until it wasn't.

"Tommy?" shouted Mom.

"See it!" he shouted back.

Tommy yanked up on the sub's joystick. Hard. The thrust of the sudden movement pinned me to the back of my seat.

I looked through the front glass of our craft. And saw the pointy tip of a long, cigar-shaped tube coated with barnacles.

"Initiate evasive maneuvers!" cried Storm.

"Already on it," Tommy replied calmly.

Our family bubble craft was rising at an extremely steep angle.

I just hoped it would be steep enough.

The pointy-tipped tube had to be some kind of bomb. We needed to clear it!

It might've been my overactive imagination, but I swear I heard the top of the bomb scraping the bottom of our submarine. I closed my eyes. If the thing exploded, we'd be back up on the surface in a flash. The kind of flash that comes with a boom.

"We're clear!" shouted Mom.

"Well done, Thomas," said Dad.

"Thanks," said Tommy, as if what he'd done was no big deal. Me? I knew I'd have to check my underpants the instant we were topside again.

Storm gestured over her shoulder at our near miss explosive device. "That's not a Russian bomb. It's what the British Royal Air Force called the Tallboy or an earthquake bomb," she informed us. "It weighs five and a half tons. Most of that is explosive material."

"I marked the location," said Mom.

"Good," said Dad, tapping the computer screen in the seatback in front of him. "I'll send the coordinates along to the proper Polish authorities."

"Um, shouldn't we wait to do that until we bring up the Amber Room?" I suggested.

"No, Bick," said Dad. "Human life over treasure. Always. An unexploded device like that is a danger to any ship that passes this way. It's also most likely leaking toxic chemicals, endangering the life of every sea creature and plant in this area. We need to immediately contact the Polish Navy and request that they defuse the bomb!"

He worked the sub's radio and sent in the message.

Tommy dipped our vessel's nose back down and took us, once again, to the sea's floor. We skirted along, swirling up sand and weedy vegetation.

"How much farther to the SS *Karlsruhe*?" Tommy asked Mom.

"Are we there yet?" asked Beck.

"Are we there yet?" I said it, too.

Beck and I are the youngest, and it's the youngest kids' job to say annoying stuff like that on family trips.

"Yes," said Mom. "We are there."

And when I squinted, I could see it, too.

The shadowy shipwreck of the sunken Nazi cargo ship was dead ahead.

CHAPTER 40

Tommy eased us closer to the ship's hull.

"There's a big gaping hole," he said. "I think we can slip through it."

"Good idea, Tommy," said Dad.

Tommy expertly maneuvered the craft. We glided along like a butter patty on ice. All that time Tommy wastes playing video games? It's given him mad joystick skills.

"Take us down to the cargo hold, Tommy," said Mom from her navigator seat.

"No problemo," said Tommy. "There's a big

elevator shaft of a hole we can use."

"Probably from where a Soviet bomb sliced through the boat and sank it," suggested Storm.

Tiny bubbles burbled up around our ship, creating a foamy curtain that blocked our view. Fortunately, the sub had all sorts of sonar and outboard sensors. It was sort of like landing an airplane in the fog. Tommy was flying blind on instruments.

There was a gentle rocking as we touched down on a deck.

The curtain of bubbles cleared. We were in an underwater warehouse filled with wooden crates and rusty military vehicles. Everything had Nazi symbols stenciled on their sides. Ugh. That'll make you shudder.

"The Amber Room's gotta be inside those wooden crates!" I said.

Dad was speechless. There was a tear welling up in the corner of his eye. Either that or our submarine had sprung a tiny leak and a water droplet had plunked into his eyeball.

"We did it," he finally said, sounding choked up.

If what we all hoped was in those crates was actually in those crates, we were very close to clearing the Kidd family name.

Closer than anybody had been since 1945. A new generation of Kidds would have found what our ancestor had, for the best of reasons, lost.

"We need to open one of those boxes," said Mom.

"Roger that," said Dad.

Then, he turned to me.

"You're up, Bick."

I slipped my hands into the glovelike devices that would allow me to manipulate and control the minisub's dual grabber claws. I'm the Kidd family champion at carnival claw-crane games. Once, at an arcade in the Netherlands, I cleaned out every single stuffed animal in the glass box. (We donated them all to a local children's hospital.)

"Easy, Bick," coached Beck as I moved the mechanical pinchers closer to the nearest crate. "Steady."

Sweat dribbled down my forehead and ski jumped off the tip of my nose. I couldn't use my hands to wipe it away so I caught it with my tongue.

"Ew, gross" was Beck's color commentary on that particular move.

I nudged a robotic hand into the rotting, sludge-crusted wood of the closest crate. The one-by-four plank, which had been underwater for decades, crumbled the instant I tapped it. I positioned my second mechanical grabber at what was left of the same slab of soggy wood. I was going to pry it free from its nails and rip the crate open so we could see what was hidden inside.

The board fell away. I grabbed hold of the one next to it. It peeled off even easier. I yanked down one more board.

Tommy powered on the submarine's high beams.

The light hit a shimmering panel of amber and gold.

"Eureka!" shouted Dad. "We found it!"

"Whoo-hoo," shouted the rest of us (including Mom).

Storm studied the thick German letters and

DO YOU NEED ANOTHER QUARTER FOR YOUR CLAW GAME, BICK?
NO THANKS. WE'RE GOOD.
CREAK!

numbers stenciled beneath the painted eagles on the sides of the crates.

"Those are instructions for putting the room back together," she said. "'Align panel A-1 above B-1.'"

Mom laughed a little. "Like putting together a bicycle on Christmas Eve."

Storm nodded. "It's the key to where all the puzzle pieces should go."

"We need to organize a proper extraction," said Dad. We could tell that he was thrilled. His grandfather Jumpin' Joe Kidd may have lost the Amber Room, but now other members of the Kidd family had found it!

Forget the goofy TV reality show competition against the Collier kids. Helping Dad score this victory made the four of us feel like the World's Greatest Treasure-Hunting Kids!

The smile on Dad's face?

It was the only prize any of us really needed.

CHAPTER 41

"Take us back to the ship, Tommy," said Dad. "We have a lot of calls to make."

"Like to Mertin Schmerkel?" said Beck. "To let him know we totally nailed the final round of the contest?"

"Sure," said Dad, sounding distracted. "We should call Schmerkel. Let him know he has a winner. But, preserving these ancient artifacts is priority one. I want to reach out to some friends. Russian antiquities experts. Let them know what we've found. They should be the ones in charge of safely retrieving the treasure. We should also contact UNESCO so they can determine the panels' permanent home."

"Um, will there be any leftover treasure we can keep for ourselves?" asked Tommy, skillfully taking us out of the cargo hold by reversing all the moves he made to bring us in.

"Not a scrap of it," said Dad. "We are sending every amber panel, every gold-gilded mirror, and every precious jewel back home to where the ICPRCP tells us it belongs."

"The icy pee?" I said.

"Did someone tinkle on a glacier?" added Beck.

Dad chuckled. So did Mom. Then Storm broke down the acronym for us.

"The ICPRCP is the Intergovernmental Committee for Promoting the Return of Cultural Property. To the countries of origin in most cases."

"Don't forget," said Mom, "the original Amber Room was a gift from the king of Prussia to the Russian czar."

"And we won't be taking any 'gifts' for ourselves," Dad said firmly.

Tommy nodded. "That's what I thought. But an amber pinky ring would look so cool. Especially if there was, like, a mosquito fossil frozen inside it."

"Not gonna happen," said Dad.

"Drop it, Tommy," added Mom.

Tommy dropped it. He also carefully piloted us through the dark and dreary waters. Schools of fish scooted out of our way. Clumps of weedy stuff swirled in our wake. We all had our noses pressed up against the curved glass of the sub's sides because we were still on the lookout for unexploded bombs or mines. Just because we'd bumped into one on the way down didn't mean there wouldn't be another one on the way up!

Finally, after what felt like forever, I saw sun dappling the water above us. We were approaching the surface.

"Excellent," said Storm, breathing a sigh of relief. "We didn't blow up."

Yep. Like I said, Storm has zero filter. She says what she's thinking whenever she happens to be thinking it.

The minisub bobbed up through the choppy water and was gently rocked by the rolling waves of the Baltic Sea.

That's when we saw them.

The ships. And boats. And helicopters.

All of them circling around *our* ship, *The Lost Again.*

"Who are all these people?" said Mom, quickly surveying the scene.

"It's probably the TV crew!" I said excitedly. "They know we won!"

"Really?" said Beck. "How could they know we won when they didn't even know exactly where we went looking for the treasure?"

"They're TV people!" I said. "They know everything. That's why they write scripts."

"No way could they know where we were," Beck countered.

"Then how'd they find us?" I snapped back.

"Maybe they traced Dad's message about the unexploded bomb to the Polish authorities."

"He used an encrypted code!"

"Did not!"

"Did, too!"

Yes, we were about to Twin Tirade in the very cramped confines of the minisub. Our hot breath was already steaming up the windows.

"You guys?" said Storm, cutting us off. She'd activated the minisub's long-range video camera. "I can see Mertin Schmerkel. He's on the deck of the biggest boat."

"See?" I said to Beck. "He's here to award us the grand prize."

"I don't think so," said Storm. "He's wearing some kind of military uniform. And all the sailors on all those ships? They're wearing uniforms and carrying weapons. Okay. Now they're not just

carrying them. They're pointing the weapons at us." She peered at the video monitor. "One might be a rocket launcher. Or a bazooka..."

Beck and I leaned in to stare at the screen, too.

"What's that strange flag they're flying?" asked Beck. "It has a black eagle sticking out its tongue and waving a sword."

"That," said Storm, "is the royal flag of Prussia."

CHAPTER 42

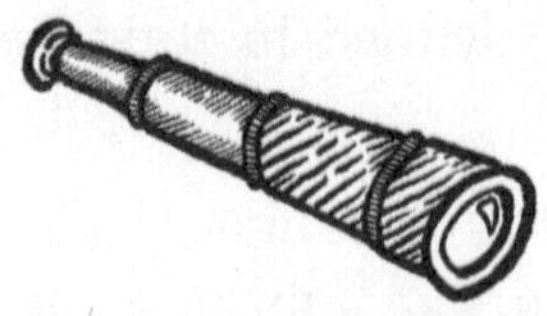

"Thomas?" Mom wondered aloud. "What's going on?"

Dad shook his head. "I'm not sure, Sue."

Suddenly, a full-scale submarine surfaced alongside Schmerkel's command ship.

There was an Nathan Collier Treasure Extractors logo painted on the side of its conning tower.

"Collier!" we all said at the same time.

And, yes, we all spit out the *k* sound.

"What should I do, Dad?" asked Tommy. "Dive back down to the shipwreck?"

Dad shook his head. "No. That'd just lead them closer to the treasure. Any evasive action could prove dangerous. We don't know what other bombs are under the water. And I wouldn't be surprised if some of their boats are equipped with anti-submarine depth charges and torpedoes."

"They'd blow us out of the water faster than that bomb we scraped past," said Tommy, reluctantly agreeing with Dad's assessment of the situation.

"And if they didn't," said Mom, "Nathan Collier would just follow after us in *his* submarine."

"Yeah," I said. "It's what he does best."

Beck nodded. "We find the treasures. He follows along after us to snatch them away."

Mom and Dad exchanged a knowing glance when Beck said that.

"So that's what this whole thing was about," mumbled Dad.

"There was never going to be a TV show," Mom mumbled back.

"Sure there was," I said. "We were the stars. Remember?"

"We won the second round?" added Beck.

Now Storm was shaking her head. "This whole thing was a complex and clever ruse. A hoax. A way to trick us into locating the Amber Room for Nathan Collier, his four kids, and Mertin Schmerkel."

"I suspect that's why someone made certain you kids found that photograph of Grandpa Joe," said Dad. "To spur you on. To make sure you'd give this final quest everything you've got."

"Collier wanted us to do all the genuine treasure hunting," said Storm. "Again."

"Collier!" was all Beck and I added to the conversation. But we really hocked out that *k* sound.

Dad put a hand on Tommy's shoulder. "Tommy? Take us over to Schmerkel and Collier. We need to find out what's going on."

"Knowledge is power," said Mom. "When we know what we're up against, we'll be better able to fight back."

"I think we're up against the Prussian Armada," said Storm. "Schmerkel is dressed like an admiral commanding a small fleet. I count a dozen ships, all of them flying the Royal Prussian flag."

"Um, I thought Prussia didn't exist anymore," said Tommy.

"It doesn't," said Mom. "At least not officially."

We puttered over to what looked like Schmerkel's command ship.

One of the Prussian sailor dudes whipped out a small whistle, what they call a boatswain's pipe, and tooted a short, shrill tune on it. It was very nautical.

We opened both side hatches on our bubble boat.

Mertin Schmerkel clicked his heels together and did a short, sharp head bob at us.

"Thank you, Kidd Family Treasure Hunters," said the slimy Nathan Collier, who'd somehow oozed his way on board Schmerkel's vessel. "You have once again led me to a very valuable treasure, which I will now remove from the ocean floor."

"Sorry, Collier," said Dad. "The Amber Room is going to be turned over to the United Nations. They will be the ones to decide who takes possession of it."

"No," said Schmerkel. "It belongs where it was created. It belongs in Prussia!"

"Um, Prussia doesn't exist anymore," said Tommy, using his helpful voice.

Schmerkel gave him a nasty, walrus-whiskers, sizzling look. I thought his monocle was going to pop out of its socket.

"Prussia shall rise again!" Schmerkel declared. "Like the phoenix bird, the black eagle will emerge from the ashes to once again rule the world."

"Prussia never actually ruled the world," said Storm. "Sure, it had a very well-organized and effective army..."

"And we will again!" declared Schmerkel. "The Amber Room will bring us enormous wealth."

"Minus, of course, my ten percent finder's fee," said Collier with a cocky smirk.

"Pah," said Schmerkel. "A mere pittance. And

you, my friend Nathan, have earned every penny of it."

"Thank you, Mertin," said Collier, clicking his heels and bowing slightly. "But I couldn't have done it without the Kidd kids." He smiled down at me. "That jumbo-sized hammer you kept as a trophy of your glorious triumph in round two? It has a highly sophisticated tracking device baked into it. It told us precisely where you were headed. All we had to do was follow its signal. That evasive, zigzag course you took? Total waste of time."

"That's the only way you know how to find treasure!" Beck shouted up at Collier. "Let us find it first."

Collier shrugged. "True. Works every time. If it ain't broke, don't fix it."

"Who engineered that tracking device?" asked Tommy. "Your brainy daughter Kioni?"

"Daughter?" said Collier. "What daughter? I don't have a daughter."

CHAPTER 43

"Uh, hello," said Storm. "Earth to Collier. Your daughter Kioni? The one who thinks she's smarter than me."

"Oh. Right. Her." Collier slapped his forehead with the palm of his hand. "I'd almost completely forgotten about her. She could play smart pretty well. So long as our team of highly paid academic advisers fed her the right information and data dumps."

Collier tapped his right ear.

"She was wearing a two-way communications device the whole time." Now Collier waggled a finger at Storm and smiled.

"You are very hard to keep up with, Stephanie Kidd."

Storm was about to explode like an undersea munition somebody just bumped into. Nobody calls her Stephanie unless *their* names are Mom or Dad.

"Excuse me," said Tommy, who probably still had some kind of tailspinning crush on Kioni Collier. "You almost forgot about your own daughter? If you ask me, Kioni Collier is totally unforgettable."

Collier tossed back his head and laughed. "Ah, ha, ha, ha."

Schmerkel tossed back his head and laughed, too! "Ah, ha, ha, ha!"

"What's so funny?" I shouted.

"Where are your kids?" added Beck. "Where are Kirk, Kioni, Carlos, and Kaiyo?"

"Yeah," I said. "We beat them, fair and square! We found the Amber Room before they did!"

"We won the competition!" added Tommy. "Even if, you know, you're stealing the treasure."

Schmerkel shook his head. "There was no

competition." He gestured to the Baltic Sea. "There was never going to be a TV show. This was the only prize we were interested in. The Amber Room! The treasure that will finance Prussia's triumphant return to the world stage."

"And, sorry," said Collier. "Those four brats aren't my children. They were actors and social media influencers. We found them at an open casting call in Hollywood. We made up those names—Kirk, Kioni, Carlos, and Kaiyo—because they sounded good with Collier."

We'd been tricked. Fooled. Bamboozled, big time.

All because we were jealous of the glamorous YouTube stars who really didn't do anything except look good on camera.

Collier grinned a sinister grin. "My children, as you call them, are all on their way home to, as the one we called Carlos put it, 'find their next gigs and create content for their socials.' I just canceled their contracts with NCTE. They won't be doing any more YouTube videos with me. But, don't worry. They're all extremely talented. They'll find new outlets for their...'creativity.' In fact, Kaiyo, whose real name is Tiffany, has already landed a role on a new sitcom. She plays the snarky one."

"She's good at that," said Storm. "A natural."

Schmerkel turned his wrist to examine his watch. "We are wasting precious time, Nathan. Enough with the chitchat, plot reveals, and gloating. We must move along to the treasure-extracting phase of our day. Remember, we Prussians prize diligence, punctuality, and efficiency."

“Of course!” said Collier. “I will organize the treasure-removal team, immediately.”

“No!” said Dad. “We found the treasure. It is ours to extract! We will assemble a team of—”

“Never!” shouted Schmerkel. “This charade is over. You and your family are hereby eliminated from the game board. You will not play on with Pleyon. I am pulling your plug, Kidd Family Treasure Hunters. You are all out of lives. Schafer?”

One of the sailors snapped to. “Yes, sir?”

“Escort these six nincompoops back to their ship. Lash them to the masts. Expose them to the elements. Make sure they are baking in the sun with no access to food or fresh water or any communication devices. They have all served their purposes for Prussia. They will not be allowed to interfere with our grand and glorious plans! Our grand and glorious future!”

PART THREE

FROM PRUSSIA, WITHOUT LOVE

CHAPTER 44

Mertin Schmerkel's new Prussian Navy had a lot of goons in its ranks.

Enough to lash the six of us to the masts and railings of our ship, lickety-split.

We were all on deck, sizzling in the sun. We were helpless. And hungry. Really hungry. I kept wishing we had packed some snacks on the submarine.

"So this is where our story ends," Nathan Collier sneered in Dad's face as two of Schmerkel's flunkies tightened the ropes restraining Dad's wrists and ankles to the mizzenmast. Collier moved back a foot or two so he could be spotlighted by a brilliant sunbeam as he threw open his arms to make a grand pronouncement.

"This was your final treasure hunt, Kidd Family Treasure Hunters. I thank you for all your efforts on my behalf and look forward to taking full credit for retrieving the Amber Room. Credit and glory is so much more fun than effort and exertion. Glory without even breaking a sweat is so, so sweet!"

"Too bad this will be your final treasure hunt, too!" I shouted at Collier.

"Yeah, Collier," cried Beck. "Without us, you couldn't find the floor if you fell out of bed!"

Ooh. That was a good one. So, I took a shot, too. "You couldn't find your butt with two hands and a map!"

"You couldn't find the tiny toy treasure inside a Kinder Surprise Egg," said Beck with the topper. "Or in a box of Cracker Jack. Or those Candy Treasure Konz. Those are delicious."

Suddenly, I was even hungrier.

"Face it, Mr. Collier," seethed Storm. "Without us, your treasure-hunting days are over, too." Her glare was so fierce, it would make anyone sweat. Too bad Collier was sweating already.

"Fine!" proclaimed Collier. "If this is to be my final quest, so be it! Schmerkel is paying me enough to retire quite comfortably. I'm thinking Iowa. Someplace in the middle of America, far away from any oceans. I hate boats. And scuba diving. And all that other stuff you Kidds have done so well for me for so many years. I bid you all adieu." He gave us a tip of his captain's hat. "Until we meet again. No. Wait. That's never going to happen. There will be no more meeting. You are all going to die out here on the Baltic Sea. No one will ever know you found the treasure your ancestor lost at the end of World War II. In a day or two, I'll give that kid Carlos the scoop about your untimely demises. He can blast your death all over his social media. He has quite a following. We'll tell him to blame pirates. I'm sure Carlos will be delighted to have the exclusive. And marauding pirates always make good clickbait."

"We're done here," snarled one of the Prussian sailors. He gestured to where a large vessel outfitted with a crane was hoisting waterlogged crates up from the shipwreck. "We should go back to assist with the treasure-recovery operation."

"Can't we go to lunch instead?" whined Collier as he and the sailors boarded a small skiff tied off to the bow of *The Lost Again*. "I'm starving. And no more borscht. I can't stand beet soup. It's making my skin turn red..."

They zoomed away, churning up a foamy triangle in their wake.

I felt terrible. I was the one who, not so long ago, had whined out loud, *That should be us on YouTube!* when I saw the fake Collier kids pretending to be treasure hunters. Now, they were getting canceled and so were we. We wouldn't be doing anything. Except getting deep-fried to a crackly crunch by the broiling sun!

BECK? COULD YOU CHANGE THAT TO A SUNSET? IT'S A BETTER WAY TO SAY 'THE END!'
ALSO, I WOULD'NT BE SWEATING SO MUCH.
YES, YOU WOULD.

CHAPTER 45

For several long, scorching hours, we watched Schmerkel's navy haul up one crate after another from the bottom of the Baltic Sea.

Beck and I were lashed pretty close together on the deck of *The Lost Again* and, since we were hot and hangry (that's hunger combined with anger), it felt like the perfect time to launch into Twin Tirade number 2,134. Hey, we had nothing better to do besides, you know, work on our final tans.

"I can't believe you fell for their act!" I snapped.

"Whose act?" Beck snapped back.

"Those Collier kids! No way were they legit treasure hunters!"

"Um, hello, Bickford. I don't remember you

calling them phonies, either!"

"Because it's rude to call someone a phony out loud or in public."

"It's also rude to smell like boiled onions mixed with rancid cheese, but you and your armpits do it all the time!"

"And it's rude for you to mention it!"

"No, it's just my survival instinct kicking in!"

"Where'd it kick you? In your brain?"

"No, your butt!"

"How could *your* instinct kick me?!?"

"Bick?" said Dad.

"Beck?" said Mom.

"Save your energy, guys," said Tommy. "As entertaining as your Twin Tirades often are, we don't have any water. And all the food is down below. In the galley." His gaze dropped to the deck beneath his feet. "Everything we need to make fluffernutters. And waffles. And those egg-in-a-hole toast things that Storm calls egg-with-a-hat and Dad says are eggs-on-an-island and Mom—"

Suddenly, off in the distance, a ship's horn blew. We heard a taut steel cable grinding to a halt on its winch. Heavy chains rattled. I squinted to the west where the sun, mercifully, was starting to take its daily dip into the sea. The new Prussian Navy hauled up its anchors. Their retrieval mission was complete. They had the Amber Room, all boxed up and ready to be put back together like the world's rarest and most expensive jigsaw puzzle.

"Thank you, once again, Kidd Family Treasure Hunters," boomed Mertin Schmerkel's voice through an amplified megaphone. "We never could have retrieved Prussia's most valuable treasure without you."

There was a screech of a squeal as someone grabbed the megaphone from Schmerkel.

"The glory will be mine!" It was Nathan Collier. "All mine! The new, reestablished country of Prussia will put my face on a postage stamp!"

I heard a rumble of laughter as all the boats in the small fleet throttled up their engines. The ships sailed off toward the sunset.

"Sorry," I said to Beck when they slipped beyond the horizon.

"Yeah," she replied. "Me, too."

We'll relabel our most recent Twin Tirade as 2,134-and-a-half. It never really got off the ground. It was sort of like a fireworks rocket with a wet fuse. It fizzled out on the launchpad.

"Kids?" said Mom. "Your father and I want you to know how proud we are of all of you!"

Uh-oh. I didn't like the sound of this. It had the feeling of a fond farewell. The last one we'd ever say to one another.

"The way you four took over *The Lost* after I went missing in the tropical storm?" said Dad, shaking his head proudly. "Amazing work, guys. Amazing."

"And then," said Mom, "you went to Egypt. Adventured down the Nile..."

"And don't forget all the incredible clues and secrets you uncovered in China!" said Dad, picking up the thread.

"Oh," said Mom, "then there was the peril we all faced at the top of world! The North Pole!"

"And our quest for the City of Gold!" added Tommy.

"And our all-American adventure!" laughed Beck.

"And all that plunder down under!" I chimed in.

We all looked to Storm, thinking she'd join in, maybe say something about our most recent escapades, battling a new version of the medieval Knights Templar all over Europe and down in Israel. But she didn't say anything. In fact, it looked like she was holding her breath.

And wiggling.

CHAPTER 46

"Storm, honey?" said Mom. "Are you okay?"

"Yeppers," she said. "But, unlike the rest of my family, I'm a little more focused on the future instead of the past!"

She triumphantly raised both her hands and pumped two fists in the air like a champion boxer.

Storm rubbed her wrists, which were still a little raw from rope burns.

"Earlier today," she said, tossing off the ropes that had been binding her, "when I noticed that Collier and Schmerkel's troops planned to lash us to the masts old-school style with ropes, I remembered a classic Navy SEAL technique for escaping in such a situation."

Mom and Dad were both beaming.

"Of course you did!" said Mom.

"Atta girl, Steph!" added Dad.

Now Storm was the one grinning from ear to ear. "It starts while they are tying you up. When they came over to strap me against this post, I tensed all my muscles and took in a very deep, chest expanding breath. Once they were finished, I relaxed and my bonds were immediately looser." She bent over to unknot the rope hobbling her ankles. "I would've freed myself sooner, but I was afraid one or more of Schmerkel's minions might've noticed and thwarted my efforts."

Storm shook her legs. The final rope flopped to the deck. She was free.

She moved over to Tommy and untied his knots in a flash because, of course, she knew how to do that, too. First she used the spoon on her Swiss Army knife to tap a knot.

"Hammering the knots loosens them. Next, I need to locate the loops and pry them apart. I then twist a loose end and push it through the knot. Finally, I insert this fork tine from my Swiss Army device's tableware assortment, gain leverage, and pull the knot apart. A marlinspike, of course, is what sailors often use to loosen tight and gnarly knots. But, marlinspikes are typically six- to twelve-inch-long metal pins and do not collapse neatly into a pocket knife."

Once Tommy was free (and found our spare marlinspike), the rest of us were out of our hemp shackles in no time. The first thing we did was race downstairs to the galley to guzzle gallons of water and gobble salty snacks. I also made myself one of those fried-eggs-inside-toast things. (That's my name for them.)

When we were all feeling a little more like ourselves, Beck turned to Mom and Dad.

"Now, what are we going to do to set things right?" she demanded.

"Chya," said Tommy. "They stole our treasure."

I nodded glumly. "They stole our glory!"

Mom and Dad both gave us the serene smiles they always have when they're cooking up a clever plan.

"We will do," said Mom, "what we always try to do."

"Exactly," said Dad. "We will do what needs to be done for our deeds to be useful."

Riiiight, I thought. *Just like that Latin motto.*

"*Nisi utile est quod facimus*," said Storm, "*stulta est gloria.*"

"Unless what we do is useful," said Beck, translating.

"Glory is foolish," I said, completing the phrase. (It's another twin thing.)

Then Beck and I looked into each other's eyes with renewed determination.

It was time to get useful.

CHAPTER 47

First, we fired up our engines and laid in a course for the coast of Poland.

While Tommy and Dad manned the helm, the rest of us raced belowdecks for that day's homework assignment: a biographical sketch of Mertin Schmerkel. To defeat your enemy, it's always good to know everything you can about them first!

Turns out that, thanks to the enormous worldwide popularity of Pleyon Games Inc., Schmerkel was the wealthiest person in all of Poland.

"That explains how he could afford his Prussian costume, all the henchpeople, and an armada of ships," said Mom.

"And," said Storm, "he might have bought a lot of

official protection back home. Wealthy billionaires like Schmerkel often make sizable campaign contributions to politicians and government officials."

"That's why we have to deal with him ourselves," said Dad. "We don't know who else we can trust."

"But," added Mom, "we can always trust family!"

The area of Poland Schmerkel called home used to be part of Prussia.

"Wow," said Storm, her fingers tap-dancing across a computer keyboard, "he has a castle!"

"Cool," I said, because I couldn't resist.

SCHMERKEL FAMILY CASTLE

Come on, wouldn't you want to live in a castle if you couldn't live on a boat?

"I bet that's where he's headed!" said Beck.

I nodded. "I know that's where I'd go if I wanted to declare myself king of Prussia. Kings love castles."

"King of Prussia is also the name of a small town in the greater Philadelphia region of Pennsylvania," said Storm, for no reason except that, maybe, that factoid had just flitted across her brain that very instant. "It's famous for its very large shopping mall. And generous food portions."

"Um, could we focus on the castle?" said Beck.

"Totally," said Storm, tapping more keys. "Mom? I am sending you the castle's GPS coordinates. Perhaps you can share them with some of your former colleagues at...*the company*?" she said with a wink and a nod.

Mom understood. She and Dad used to work for the CIA. They still had a ton of spy friends and spook colleagues at "the company," as Storm called it. And some of those folks had access to spy satellites! They'd feed us intel without asking too many questions. Which was a good thing, because they weren't family, either.

Storm also relayed the coordinates of Schmerkel's castle up to Dad and Tommy on the bridge. They now had a better idea about where precisely on the Polish coast we should be navigating toward.

I felt *The Lost Again* lunge forward.

Up in the wheelhouse, they'd definitely plotted the new course and were gunning for it, full speed ahead!

Maybe ten minutes after Mom contacted her old friends in the spy craft trade, she asked Storm to slide away from the computer. It was Mom's turn to tickle the keyboard.

"Here we go," she said as a live, overhead video image appeared on the screen. "There's a long convoy of trucks heading toward Schmerkel's castle."

"Trucks carrying the crates filled with the treasures of the Amber Room," said Storm.

"Exactly."

"Then that's where we need to be, too!" I said, pounding my fist into my open palm for emphasis.

"Totally!" said Beck. She pounded her fist into my open palm, too.

Her punch stung way worse than mine.

CHAPTER 48

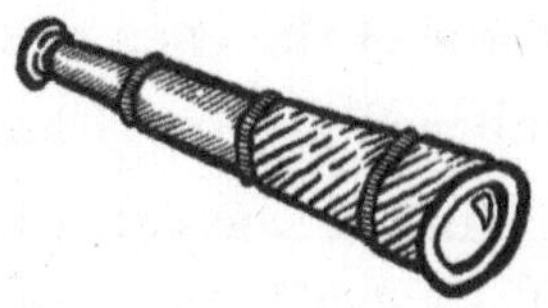

A car was waiting for us when we landed on the Polish coast.

And it wasn't an Uber. It was a hulking SUV with tinted windows. The kind foreign dignitaries ride in on their way to do dignified stuff. We all climbed in with our go bags and assorted espionage gear. When your parents are both former spies, you have a lot of that sort of stuff lying around the house or, in our case, the boat.

The driver, who had a serious buzz cut and an "I just gargled with vinegar" scowl, didn't say much. But, what he said, he said in a thick and mysterious accent.

"I have received my instructions," he told us.

"In. Everybody. Now. And, if anybody asks, I was never here."

Oh, yeah. The spooky dude was definitely a spy. Hopefully, one of the ones on our side.

We all clambered aboard. I happened to have the middle seat in the second row of the SUV so I could eyeball the driver in the rearview mirror.

"The one who sits between two chairs may easily fall down," I said to him with a knowing nod. I was hoping to confirm his secret agent-ness by talking like spies do in the movies.

It didn't work. The guy didn't even blink. Although his jaw joint did seem to bulge a little. He might've been chewing gum.

It was dark when the mysterious driver dropped us off. He didn't wish us good luck. He just reminded us that we'd never met him and drove away.

We made our way through a stand of trees, following the blinking green dot on Mom's mapping device. Soon, the silhouette of Schmerkel's castle emerged. We could see it looming in the distance, on the far side of a very spiky fence and a wide-open lawn. Not many windows were illuminated.

“This is the rear of the building,” whispered Dad. “All the invited guests use the front door.”

“Then this is the entrance for us,” said Storm.

Tommy tried a nearby gate. It wasn’t locked.

“He probably has guard dogs,” said Mom. “No need to lock up if you have German shepherds and Dobermans on patrol.”

“It’s at least a hundred yards to the castle,” said Tommy, using a small scope to survey the surroundings.

Suddenly, I heard a chorus of meows behind us.

Feral cats. A whole colony of them. They looked hungry. I wondered if our ankles looked appetizing to them.

“Tommy?” I whispered. “Did you pack your hacky sack ball?”

“It’s not a ball, little bro. It’s a footbag filled with plastic pellets.”

“It’s a ball!” said Beck. “A beanbag ball!”

“Okay, okay. It’s a ball.”

“Who else has snacks in their go bags?” I asked.

Everybody's hands shot up. After baking in the sun without food or water, we'd all loaded up.

"I grabbed some of those miniature cheeses I like," said Beck.

"Me, too," said Mom.

"Perfect," I said. "Unwrap the wax. Smear the cheese on Tommy's hacky sack thing."

"What are you thinking, Bickford?" wondered Dad.

"That he wants me to go hungry no matter how long this mission lasts!" replied Beck.

I shook my head. "Cats like cheese. Dogs like cats. If Tommy can fling his cheese-coated ball one way..."

"The hungry cats will chase after it!" said Dad. "The guard dogs will chase after the cats, buying us enough time to make it to that service door." He pointed out his target with the red dot of a laser pointer.

The feral cats meowed. And purred. They were at full alert. Tracking Dad's laser.

"Forget the cheeseball!" said Beck. "Just use your laser pointer, Dad!"

"Excellent suggestion, Rebecca!" Dad repositioned his red dot at the far edge of the sweeping lawn. Then he jiggled it around a little.

The cats went cuckoo!

They tore through the fence posts. They swarmed across the grass.

In the distance, we could hear dogs snarl and bark.

Then, they blasted off to chase the cats.

The instant the dogs passed our position, we flew through the gate and ran across the open

MY IDEA WAS A LOT LESS CHEESY THAN BICK'S.

field! Dad kept luring the cats to the far corner of the castle with his laser pointer, even as he ran. The guy's a real multitasker.

When we neared the castle's clearly marked SERVICE ENTRANCE, Mom disabled the closest security camera with a blast of a bright LED flashlight. Storm jammed its transmission signal with this black box thingy she'd built. No one would be tracking us.

Dad used his lock-picking tools on the service entrance door.

We slid inside and crept deeper into the creepy stone fortress. No one was in the kitchen. Or the butler's pantry.

Up ahead, we heard voices. And laughter. And military music. It sounded like Mertin Schmerkel was hosting a party!

Of course he was.

It was a victory celebration.

CHAPTER 49

We tiptoed up a sweeping set of stairs to a balcony above a large, cavernous hall.

The grand ballroom below was decorated with banners and bunting and tons of Prussian flags. Empty knights-in-shining-armor suits stood at rigid attention on the ledges of nooks filled with soaring stained-glass windows, all of which featured a very heroic-looking Mertin Schmerkel in various triumphant poses—monocle included.

We dropped to our knees and worked our way across the plush carpet to the three-foot-tall balcony wall. Fortunately, all of our go bags included miniature spy periscopes. Beck and I had toy plastic ones but, hey, they worked.

Down below, I could see all sorts of fancy people dressed in formal wear and military uniforms. Old-fashioned military uniforms. The kind the Prussians might've worn back in like 1870. Some of the ladies were wearing powdered white wigs. Some of the men, too!

I wanted to capture this bizarro scene on video. So, after making sure it was muted, I positioned my phone over my periscope viewing slot and started recording. Now I could watch Schmerkel and his cronies on a screen. (I also wouldn't wind up with an eyepiece circle ringing my eye like a pink monocle.)

"My fellow Prussians," Schmerkel said to the gathered throng, raising a crystal goblet of something bubbly. "Tonight, we celebrate the first step in our long march to reclaim our former glory. I have, with the help of the Nathan Collier Treasure Extractors company—"

Collier, who was dressed in a tailcoat and matching black captain's hat, stepped forward through the crowd. He raised a crisp business card. "I am available for all your future treasure-hunting needs," he said. Then he mimed putting a phone to his ear with his thumb and pinky. "Call me," me mouthed to the crowd.

Ha, I thought. *Future treasure hunts? Without us Kidds, Collier couldn't even dig up earwax with a cotton swab the size of a steam shovel.*

Schmerkel cleared his throat. I think that's how Prussian people tell other people to stop talking. Collier took the hint.

"As I was saying," Schmerkel continued, "I have retrieved our nation's sacred treasure from the bottom of the Baltic Sea." He gestured to a row of wooden crates lined up against one wall. Most of them had the markings giving instructions on how to piece the Amber Room back together. Some had other markings. Hard to say what might be in those boxes.

"And so," said Schmerkel, "tonight, we celebrate the return of the Amber Room, the Eighth Wonder of the World, to its proper home. Prussia! Six tons of amber! One hundred and twenty-nine bejeweled panels! All of it has come home to the fatherland!"

DO YOU LIKE MY POWDERED WIG?
MADAM, I PREFER POWDERED DONUTS.
OR FUNNEL CAKES.

His audience pitter-pattered their white-gloved hands in applause.

Schmerkel clasped his hands behind his back and swaggered forward on his elevated platform.

"Never forget, my friends, that this marvelous masterpiece was created by skilled Prussian craftsmen right here in Prussia. Oh, what a pity that, in 1716, our deluded King Friedrich Wilhelm decided to pack up the Amber Room into eighteen crates and send it as a gift to that loser Czar Peter the Great of Russia. Great? Pah! He was mediocre at best!"

"Pah!" echoed the crowd.

"Peter the Loser!" shouted Collier.

Schmerkel chuckled. That gave permission for his guests to chuckle, too.

He let them do that for about fifteen seconds. Then, he raised both of his beefy hands to silence them. I zoomed in for a close-up.

"Soon," said Schmerkel, "our good friend and coconspirator, Nathan Collier..."

Collier did that thumb-and-pinky "call me" thing again.

"...will help us melt down all this amber and the gold. We will pluck the jewels from the panels. We will sell it all to the highest bidders and, without a doubt, raise enough money to finance the new Prussia! We will no longer be part of, pah, Poland!"

"Pah, Poland!" echoed his crowd. A lot them spat at the floor with whatever they'd been sipping when they did the *pah* and the *P* in Poland.

"We will no longer be vassals and serfs subject to the whims of our Polish overlords! We will, once again, be our own great and mighty country! Prussia! The most feared soldiers on earth!"

CHAPTER 50

Suddenly, Dad's periscope device dipped down.

By the way, he and Mom have the high-tech, super-sleek aluminum ones that real spies use to see around corners. They weren't working with the plastic pipe number that comes with the Sneaky Surveillance toy kit like me and Beck. Tommy had a cardboard box contraption. Storm's? Well, she designed it. I can't describe it.

"What's up?" Mom whispered to Dad when both their devices were down.

"Text," Dad whispered back, using that clipped and efficient tone he uses when he is in super stealthy mode. "UN contact. The Polish help we requested? No go."

Dad thumbed his device and forwarded us all the text he'd just received from a friend at the United Nations. None of our phones dinged. They'd been silenced long ago. When you're a Kidd kid, you know how to follow your parents' super stealthy example.

I read the text:

> Thomas, I regret to inform you that the Polish authorities are not worried about Mr. Mertin Schmerkel or what he might have brought up from the bottom of the Baltic Sea. They say he is not a threat; he is simply a treasure hunter. They wish him well in all his future endeavors. They also suggested that I play on with Pleyon. Sorry. Thank you for all you continue to do (or attempt to do) for UNESCO.

The subtext of the text was crystal clear: some very high-level, high-powered Polish officials and authorities were clearly in debt to billionaire tech mogul Mertin Schmerkel. No way were they going to turn on him.

That meant we were totally on our own. The only thing that stood in the way of Schmerkel's plans to destroy the Amber Room, the Eighth Wonder of the World, was us, the Kidds. And we were all currently crawling around on a ballroom balcony on our hands and knees, playing with our periscopes.

"Sir?" we heard a voice ring out from the ballroom. It was followed by the crisp click of bootheels. "The melting pots in the smelting chamber below have reached the desired temperature of one hundred and seventy-five degrees Celsius. On your command, we will smash, I mean, granulate the amber from the panels and then subject the heated material to five hundred kilograms of pressure. We will mass-produce amber bricks!"

"No," said Storm, sounding shocked—even without raising her voice. "Those techniques will ruin the gemstone."

"Excellent!" cried Schmerkel, who hadn't

heard Storm. "Let us transport these crates to the cellar and initiate the removal and...*granulation*... of the panels. It is time the Amber Room had a... meltdown!"

He snickered at his own little pun. So, the rest of the ballroom snickered, too.

"Come on," said Dad. "We need to be down in that ballroom. Now."

Mom nodded. "We have to talk them out of taking a sledgehammer to the Amber Room."

"Chya," said Tommy. "And I need to meet that young baroness in the sparkly green gown. What's she doing hanging out with all those dusty old dudes? That's the real crime going on down in that ballroom."

"Bick and Beck?" said Dad. "Stay up here."

"Why?" we both said at the same time.

"Because we said so," said Mom, falling back on one of the oldest parental fallbacks in the world.

"Fine!" I said.

Beck looked to me. I gave her a small nod.

She understood.

We had to stay up in the balcony just in case

Mom, Dad, Storm, and Tommy totally failed at persuading the Prussians to do the right thing. The saber-rattlers down in the ballroom were true fanatics. Things like reason, science, and the proper way to handle amber probably weren't big on their list of priorities. They were more focused on other stuff. Like waxing their mustaches, chortling "moo-ha-ha," and ruling the world from their evil lair.

So Beck and I hung back.

Mom, Dad, Tommy, and Storm charged down the staircase to confront Schmerkel.

"Schmerkel?" boomed Dad when he reached the ballroom. "Don't touch those crates!"

CHAPTER 51

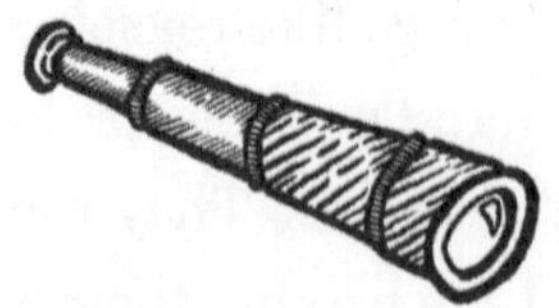

"You fools dare interrupt my triumphant celebration?" Schmerkel shouted at Dad.

"It's for your own good!" said Dad.

"And the good of the Amber Room!" said Mom.

"Tell them about how they're going to ruin the gemstone, sis," said Tommy. "She's smart. Me? I'm just this good looking...all the time." He winked at the young baroness in the sparkly green gown.

Storm started explaining how the amber could be ruined if subjected to intense heat. "Amber, you should know, is not actually a stone. It is fossilized tree resin. Melted incorrectly, it could end up decomposing. Turning it into something closer to asphalt than precious jewelry..."

While Storm droned on with the boring details, Beck started the second half of Twin Tirade 2,134. It was our first silent one. All texts. But the thumbs were flying.

First, she hit me up with a few furious face emojis and that nasty one that isn't a cup of soft serve chocolate ice cream.

Oh, yeah. She was mad we were left behind.

So, I fired back with a smiley face and a unicorn, just to make her madder.

"This is so ridiculous!" she wrote with a frantic barrage of tippity-taps on her screen.

"So's that thing in your hair, but do you hear me complaining?" I tapped back.

"It's called a scrunchie, Bick."

"Really? Because that's what I call your face."

"I only make that scrunched-up face when I smell you!"

Our texts were flying back and forth so fast and furiously, my knuckles ached. Fortunately, our Twin Tirade cooled off as quickly as it heated up.

"You really are fast with your thumbs," typed Beck.

"Your spelling is superb."

"Except when the phone thinks I'm trying to spell something else."

"I no. I ate hat."

"You mean—I know, I hate that?"

"Exactly."

"Storm is getting nowhere."

"She might be putting some of them to sleep."

"Uh-oh, Schmerkel is screaming again."

"Silence!" the would-be Prussian king declared. "Enough with the science and the blah-blah-blah. I guarantee you—no one here is interested in your jibber-jabbering about such gobbledygook and kauderwelsch!"

"Same thing," said Storm. "Gobbledygook and kauderwelsch..."

"I know that! And both will be against the law in the new Prussia. In the new Prussia, we will go with our gut, not our brain!"

This was met by a chorus of "hear, hears" and "harrumphs" and more than a few enthusiastic cane taps to the floor.

"The Polish government isn't going to like you

setting up your own nation-state, Mertin," said Mom.

"We'll expose your insurrection plans to the authorities!" added Dad.

"You'll go to jail," said Tommy.

"We have our phones!" said Mom, pulling hers out of a pocket.

That was not the best super spy move she's ever made.

"Remove their devices!" commanded Schmerkel. His goons did so. Immediately.

Mom, Dad, Tommy, and Storm didn't have a leg to stand on. We already knew that the Polish authorities weren't worried about Schmerkel. And Schmerkel wasn't worried about anybody whose last name was Kidd. Don't forget, his initial plan was to slowly roast us to death out on the Baltic Sea.

"You will not be calling anyone, foolish Kidd family. And, if you already have, if anyone attempts to storm this castle, to stop me in my noble quest, you four will be the first casualties of Prussia's new military might." We heard boots on the ballroom floor. I peeked over the edge of the balcony barrier with my periscope.

Armed soldiers had just swept in. We're talking armed with rifles, not antique swords.

"I am so sorry, Dr. Kidd," Schmerkel gloated. "No one will know of your discovery. You will never redeem the honor of your family name so besmirched by your disgraced grandfather Joseph Kidd!"

"Never!" echoed Nathan Collier. He liked a good gloat, too.

Schmerkel adjusted his monocle. I could tell: he was about to start a dramatic monologue. He'd step into the spotlight and explain to everybody how super smart and clever he was. The villains we deal with do that a lot.

But, this time I didn't mind. The blowhard's self-important speechifying would buy me some time. And I needed that time.

Because I'd just had an idea! One last-ditch effort to save the day and maybe our family's reputation, too.

CHAPTER 52

I started tapping my thumbs on the face of my phone again.

"Um, are we going to have another Twin Text Tirade?" whispered Beck.

"Nope."

"What are you doing, Bick?"

"Sending a video clip to CarlosTheCool."

"Who?"

"Carlos Collier—or whatever his real name is. He's one person who'd never turn down a juicy social media post."

"You know how to reach him?"

I nodded. "He shared his 'deets' with me, remember? Told me to hit him up if I ever had any fresh content I wanted to boost. He has a bajillion followers. I'm hoping one or two of them have parents who work for the Polish government, police, or army."

Because I had a hot scoop for TikTok, Knick-Knock, YouTube, and all of Carlos's many social media channels. All about a little Prussian Revolution in Poland. If we could expose it, make the video go viral, it'd be a chance for us to use social media for something besides being famous and scoring Likes.

I added a few hashtags. #SchmerkelCastle. #PrussianRevolution. #LookOutPoland. Then I told the message app it was more than okay for it to identify my current location. Hey, I wanted the whole world to know where I was and, more important, where Mr. Schmerkel and his minions were.

I attached my video file and hit Send.

My note was in the air. I saw the "Delivered" message come up on my screen. CarlosTheCool could now host the exclusive world premiere of my video drop. A little something I liked to call Mertin Schmerkel's Outright Rebellion Rant.

If Carlos decided he wanted to.

If my clickbait was juicy enough for him.

If it wasn't too early in the day wherever Carlos was and he was awake enough to hear his phone ding.

Yeah. There were a whole lot of *if*s. I might need a plan B. I wondered what the number for 9-1-1 was in Poland.

Meanwhile, downstairs, the wannabe king of Prussia was still blabbing.

"You see, Dr. Thomas Kidd," said Schmerkel, clearly enjoying telling this tale, "on that fateful day in 1945, a team of Prussian, or should I say *German*, commandos followed your grandfather Professor Joseph Kidd and his Russian Monuments Men colleague, Sergei, into Königsberg Castle, where they went on their search for the Amber Room. While the two academics wasted time dragging a clumsy custodian to safety, those clever Prussian Germans—okay, they were Nazis—they snuck down to the cellar and hauled out the treasure. Eighteen crates was their haul. The next day, when your grandfather and the Russian returned to the castle, whatever had been hidden in the basement was long gone. There weren't any crates. No jewel-encrusted amber panels or golden statues. It was all on board the *Karlsruhe*—the last Nazi cargo ship out of Königsberg! The one that the villainous Russians sank in the Baltic Sea."

Schmerkel descended from his miniature stage and marched up to Mom and Dad.

"And now, it is mine! All mine! Bow before your Prussian king!"

"No!" shouted Tommy, Storm, Mom, and Dad—all at the same time.

Mertin Schmerkel did not look pleased. Prussians seem big on obeying orders. I don't think anybody had dared to disagree with Schmerkel in a long, long time.

"Take them away!" shouted Schmerkel. "Throw them in the melting pots! Smelt them first."

"Those guys are in trouble down there," said Beck.

I nodded. "It's time we joined them!"

CHAPTER 53

Beck and I dashed down the curving staircase and burst into the ballroom.

I glanced at the crates lined up around the room. I did a quick count. There were twenty-four. Most of them had the markings Storm had ID'd. Instructions on which panel went where.

But some of the wooden boxes had a different series of markings and symbols.

I remember something Schmerkel had just said. About how the Amber Room had been packed into eighteen crates.

I'm no Storm, but I could do that much math. Six of the wooden crates ringing the ballroom weren't filled with amber panels. It was time for me to try something crazy. To buy more time for CarlosTheCool to post my video clip and, hopefully, rack up something besides a bunch of emojis.

"No, Mom and Dad!" I shouted. "Mr. Schmerkel is correct. The time to open these crates is now!"

I grabbed a saber out of the scabbard of the nearest old geezer. The guy nearly toppled sideways when I drew out his sword. I think he'd been using it for balance.

"Bick?" shouted Dad.

"Don't!" hollered Mom.

For the first time in my life, I didn't listen. I was actively disobeying my parents.

I tore across the room, swinging the sword over my head.

"Charge!"

"I'll be back!" Tommy said to the woman in the sparkly green gown. He was set to chase after me.

Luckily, the lady slowed him down.

"If I could rearrange the alphabet," she said in a husky voice, "I'd put *U* and *I* together."

Tommy froze. It gave me just enough time to

OFFICIAL GROUNDS FOR DIVORCING A TWIN?

reach the crate I was aiming for. I jammed the saber into a crack between wooden planks.

I heard Mom, Dad, Storm, and Beck screaming in slow motion: "Noooooooo, Biiiiiicccccckkkkk, doooooon't!"

I didn't listen to them.

I leaned against the hilt of the saber.

It was time to pop open the crate!

The board came free with the screech of rusty nails giving way. I crowbarred out another plank.

Some pots and pans clattered to the floor. They were followed by several antique tins of cured bauernbratwurst—that canned meat Tommy used to like eating when he was a kid. Guess folks liked it back in 1945, too.

"Hang on," I said, reaching into the crate. "There's no amber in here, but I see more pots and pans. And some auto parts. Anybody need a hubcap for an old armored car?"

I let that drop to the floor and wobble around.

"I see some documents, but they're all waterlogged. Oh, here's a rusty pistol. I wonder if it still works..."

Beck was the first to catch on to what I was doing.

"Oops," she said. "We dug up the wrong treasure. Do we win the contest anyhow?"

"There isn't a contest anymore," I told her. "Remember?"

"Right," says Beck.

Mom, Dad, and Storm gave Beck and me a piercing look until, yes, they figured it out, too.

They finally realized I'd purposefully pried open one of the crates without the Amber Room markings on its side to make Schmerkel and company think that none of the crates held any of the priceless panels.

Then I popped open another while Beck yanked open a third with a poker she'd grabbed from the fireplace.

Tommy and Storm helped haul out the junk stashed in it.

Furious, Schmerkel turned to glare at Collier.

"You assured me that the Amber Room was on board that ship!"

Terrified, Collier pointed a quivering finger at

Mom and Dad. "Because that's where they said it was."

"We never said that," said Mom.

"But you sent those Polish divers to the Baltic Sea!" shouted Collier.

"Because," said Dad with a sly smile, "our oldest son, Tommy, enjoys his canned meat."

"Totally," said Tommy. "That bauernbratwurst is delish."

Schmerkel stomped both of his booted feet on the dance floor. Hard. "We have wasted so much valuable time!"

All of his guests stomped their feet, too—wasting just enough more time for the Polish police to arrive. They were joined by what looked like a Polish Army battalion.

Apparently, some of their children follow CarlosTheCool on Instagram and TikTok. Maybe Snapchat, too.

Because the cavalry had arrived!

And the way they were acting? They definitely weren't on Schmerkel's payroll!

These were the good guys.

CHAPTER 54

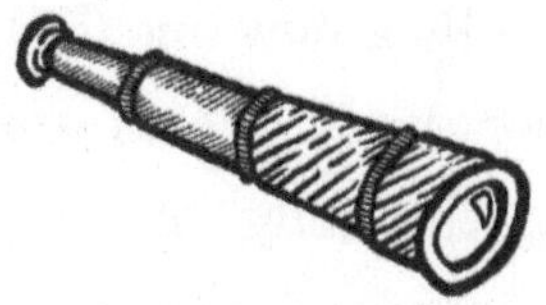

Mertin Schmerkel was clasped in handcuffs and hauled away.

He would be charged with treason. And being a traitor. And inciting insurrection, civil war, and other bad stuff.

I didn't think Mr. Schmerkel would be wearing any more Prussian uniforms where he was going. He'd probably be more of an orange jumpsuit kind of guy. And, I was pretty sure they'd confiscate his monocle, too.

Since Nathan Collier was in the crowd of the video CarlosTheCool had posted, he was being detained, too. I'd caught him in the background, whooping it up and hollering, as Schmerkel laid out his scheme for a new Prussia seceding from the old Poland. Poor Collier. He was going back to jail. At least it'd be a new one for him.

All the other party guests were hauled away, too—including the lady in the sparkly green gown. Tommy promised he'd visit her in prison.

"Unless you're, like, guilty of conspiring to overthrow your government or something."

"I am," she told him, batting her eyelashes innocently. "I'm guilty, guilty, guilty."

"Fine," said Tommy. "Then tell the judge to add another crime to your long list of charges: breaking my heart."

When all the Prussians were out of the ballroom, we Kidds had a little family meeting over by the cargo crates, which were under the watchful eye of the Polish military.

"The UNESCO folks are already talking," Dad told us. "They will work out who gets the treasure."

"Seriously?" said Tommy. "Somebody wants all those pots and pans? And what about the meat tins? Are they going to put them in a World War

II museum or something? Because, I'm kind of hungry."

"Sorry, Tommy," said Storm. "Unopened canned meat, such as Spam or corn beef, only lasts two to five years."

Tommy started counting on his fingers.

"The boat went down in 1945, Tommy!" said Beck with a laugh. "That canned meat went bad when Harry S. Truman was in the White House."

Tommy nodded grimly and accepted his fate.

"Bick?" said Mom, very proudly. "What you did was extremely clever."

"Yeah," said Beck. She even draped an arm over my shoulder. "Gonna be one of my best action scenes ever! The way you ripped open that crate with the saber was so cool! It was almost as if you were your own stunt double!"

Now Storm draped her arm over my other shoulder. "Super smart, little brother. You even outthought me."

"And under pressure, too," added Dad.

Tommy was still confused. "Um, what did Bick do?"

"I realized," I said, puffing up my chest a little, "that the Amber Room wasn't the only cargo on that sunken ship. That the priceless panels and semiprecious jewels were only in the crates with the markings for how to put the room back together. The ones Storm identified for us."

Storm nodded. "Yes. It's true. That part was all me."

"So Bick tore open a crate with different markings," said Beck, finishing my story for me. It's yet another twin thing.

"And," said Mom, "Mertin Schmerkel jumped to conclusions. He made the faulty assumption that what was true for a few crates would be true for all of them."

"Which," said Beck, "gave time for Bick's other genius idea to play out. The video he shot and sent to the hotshot influencer, Carlos not-really-a-Collier."

Wow. Beck was saying such nice stuff about me, I wondered if we'd ever get around to Twin Tirade 2,135.

CHAPTER 55

Early the next morning, Storm noticed that CarlosTheCool had put up a new post.

It was a picture of him posing in front of a large Polish flag with a wicker basket stuffed with gourmet Polish treats. Kielbasa, potato and cheese pierogi, sauerkraut and mushroom pierogi, pierogi-filled pierogi, and sunflower bread—plus Polish pickles, Polish mustard, and Polish horse-radish.

His caption was short and to the point:

> I just, like, totally saved the country of Poland, people. You're welcome.

"Guess he gets all the glory," said Beck.

"Let him have it," I said. "We know the truth. And that's all that really matters."

"Wow," said Mom.

"You've really grown up fast, young man," said Dad. They were both beaming.

I shrugged. "Guess it was all that sunshine and fresh air."

People from that United Nations ICP group arrived later in the day. Negotiations had already begun as to where the Amber Room belonged. UN scientists felt confident that the cold waters of the Baltic had preserved the panels quite well. The crates would not, however, be opened until they were in a controlled environment.

"Too bad those cold waters couldn't save the meat tins," Tommy grumbled under his breath when he heard that.

So, I guess you know how things eventually worked out.

Because you've never heard about the real Amber Room being found or going on display anywhere, have you? You might've even googled across stories that say that the cargo hold of the *Karlsruhe* shipwreck was not where the Amber Room ended up.

So, in the end, there wasn't much glory for the Kidd Family Treasure Hunters. But I wanted YOU to know the truth, even if certain grown-ups in New York City don't want you to hear it.

We found the treasure that our great-grandfather had been trying to save when it was more important for him to save a fellow human being. He didn't need any glory. Because he'd been extremely useful.

And we didn't need any glory, either.

We'd been extremely useful, too. We saved the Eighth Wonder of the World.

Even if nobody except you, loyal reader, knows we did it.

Yep, it's like that ancient Roman guy, Phaedrus, used to say back in the first century when everybody chiseled Latin stuff into marble: *Nisi utile est quod facimus, stulta est gloria.*

"Unless what we do is useful, glory is foolish."

And us Kidds? We prefer being useful to being foolish. Okay, fine. Beck says my clothes are still foolish. And my hair is downright ridiculous.

Whatever. That's it for me. It's been fun sharing these adventures with you. But now I have to go.

Beck's waiting.

We have a Twin Tirade to get started.

ALSO BY JAMES PATTERSON

MIDDLE SCHOOL SERIES

The Worst Years of My Life (*with Chris Tebbetts*)
Get Me Out of Here! (*with Chris Tebbetts*)
My Brother Is a Big, Fat Liar (*with Lisa Papademetriou*)
How I Survived Bullies, Broccoli, and Snake Hill (*with Chris Tebbetts*)
Ultimate Showdown (*with Julia Bergen*)
Save Rafe! (*with Chris Tebbetts*)
Just My Rotten Luck (*with Chris Tebbetts*)
Dog's Best Friend (*with Chris Tebbetts*)
Escape to Australia (*with Martin Chatterton*)
From Hero to Zero (*with Chris Tebbetts*)
Born to Rock (*with Chris Tebbetts*)
Master of Disaster (*with Chris Tebbetts*)
Field Trip Fiasco (*with Martin Chatterton*)
It's a Zoo in Here! (*with Brian Sitts*)
Winter Blunderland (*with Brian Sitts*)

ALI CROSS SERIES

Ali Cross
Ali Cross: Like Father, Like Son
Ali Cross: The Secret Detective

I FUNNY SERIES

I Funny (*with Chris Grabenstein*)
I Even Funnier (*with Chris Grabenstein*)
I Totally Funniest (*with Chris Grabenstein*)
I Funny TV (*with Chris Grabenstein*)
School of Laughs (*with Chris Grabenstein*)
The Nerdiest, Wimpiest, Dorkiest I Funny Ever (*with Chris Grabenstein*)

MAX EINSTEIN SERIES

The Genius Experiment (*with Chris Grabenstein*)
Rebels with a Cause (*with Chris Grabenstein*)
Saves the Future (*with Chris Grabenstein*)
World Champions! (*with Chris Grabenstein*)

TREASURE HUNTERS SERIES

Treasure Hunters (*with Chris Grabenstein*)
Danger Down the Nile (*with Chris Grabenstein*)
Secret of the Forbidden City (*with Chris Grabenstein*)
Peril at the Top of the World (*with Chris Grabenstein*)
Quest for the City of Gold (*with Chris Grabenstein*)
All-American Adventure (*with Chris Grabenstein*)
The Plunder Down Under (*with Chris Grabenstein*)
Ultimate Quest (*with Chris Grabenstein*)

DOG DIARIES SERIES

Dog Diaries (*with Steven Butler*)
Happy Howlidays! (*with Steven Butler*)
Mission Impawsible (*with Steven Butler*)
Curse of the Mystery Mutt (*with Steven Butler*)
Camping Chaos! (*with Steven Butler*)
Dinosaur Disaster! (*with Steven Butler*)
Big Top Bonanza! (*with Steven Butler*)

HOUSE OF ROBOTS SERIES

House of Robots (*with Chris Grabenstein*)
Robots Go Wild! (*with Chris Grabenstein*)
Robot Revolution (*with Chris Grabenstein*)

JACKY HA-HA SERIES

Jacky Ha-Ha (*with Chris Grabenstein*)
My Life is a Joke (*with Chris Grabenstein*)
Jacky Ha-Ha Gets the Last Laugh (*with Chris Grabenstein*)

OTHER ILLUSTRATED NOVELS

Kenny Wright: Superhero (*with Chris Tebbetts*)
Homeroom Diaries (*with Lisa Papademetriou*)
Word of Mouse (*with Chris Grabenstein*)
Pottymouth and Stoopid (*with Chris Grabenstein*)
Laugh Out Loud (*with Chris Grabenstein*)
Not So Normal Norbert (*with Joey Green*)
Unbelievably Boring Bart (*with Duane Swierczynski*)
Katt vs. Dogg (*with Chris Grabenstein*)
Scaredy Cat (*with Chris Grabenstein*)

Best Nerds Forever (*with Chris Grabenstein*)
Katt Loves Dogg (*with Chris Grabenstein*)
The Runaway's Diary *(with Emily Raymond)*
The Elephant Girl (*with Ellen Banda-Aaku and Sophia Krevoy*)

DANIEL X SERIES

The Dangerous Days of Daniel X (*with Michael Ledwidge*)
Watch the Skies (*with Ned Rust*)
Demons and Druids (*with Adam Sadler*)
Game Over (*with Ned Rust*)
Armageddon (*with Chris Grabenstein*)
Lights Out (*with Chris Grabenstein*)

For more information about James Patterson's novels,
visit www.penguin.co.uk